Paul Soboleski

Napoleon and his Marshals

Paul Soboleski

Napoleon and his Marshals

ISBN/EAN: 9783337382889

Printed in Europe, USA, Canada, Australia, Japan

Cover: Foto ©Andreas Hilbeck / pixelio.de

More available books at **www.hansebooks.com**

Napoleon Bonaparte

AND HIS MARSHALS.

OUDINOT.

OUDINOT, Charles Nicholas, duke of Reggio, Marshal and peer of France, born April 2, 1767, at Bar-sur-Ornain, of a respectable mercantile family. He entered the military service in his sixteenth year, was a zealous friend of the revolution, and distinguished himself in September, 1792, by the defence of the Castle of Bitche against the Prussians. Brave even to rashness, often and grievously wounded, he rose by brilliant actions, to the rank of general of division in 1799. He contributed much to the victory of Zurich and was chief of the staff of Massena, to whom he gave important assistance at the siege of Genoa. In 1805 Oudinot obtained the command of the new corps of grenadiers. After the taking of Vienna he obtained the possession of the bridge of Tabor by snatching a lighted match from the hands of an Austrian artillerist. In 1807 Napoleon raised him to the rank of Count. June 14, 1807, he made head against the Russian army at Friedland, until Napoleon arrived with his army to complete his victory. After the peace of Vienna, in 1809, Napoleon made him Marshal and Duke of Reggio. In 1812 he commanded the twelfth corps, was for some months governor of Berlin, fought gloriously on the Dwina and Beresina, was severely wounded, and escaped being taken only by his extraordinary courage. In the campaign of 1813, he lost (Aug. 12) the battle of Grossbeeren. He took part in the battle of Leipsic and most of the battles in 1814. After the capitulation of Paris, he declared for the provisional government. Louis XVIII appointed him Commander in Chief of the grenadiers and royal chasseurs. During the hundred days he lived on his Estate. After the second restoration the king appointed him commander of the Parisian National Guard, an office which he lost at the suppression of that body, in 1827. In 1823 he was governor of Madrid. After the revolution of 1830 he gave a steady support to the government of Louis Philippe, who appointed him in May, 1839, to the office of Grand Chancellor of the Legion of Honor, and subsequently to succeed Marshal Moncey as governor of the Hotel of the Invalids, in 1842. After the revolution of 1848 he was appointed to command the French army sent against the Roman Republic, landed at Civita Vecchia, April 25, 1849, and took possession of Rome July 3. He died in Paris soon after.

VANDAMME.

VANDAMME, Dominique, count of Unebourg, born at Cassel in 1771, was the son of an Apothecary. He owed a most rapid advancement to an almost unexampled courage. In 1792 he acted in the quality of a general of brigade. In 1799 was appointed general of division and commanded the left wing of the army of the Danube. Passed into Holland, and was successful there, distinguished himself at the passage of the Rhine, and in various memorable battles of 1800. In 1809, was very successful in campaign against Austria. On the 29th of August he was taken prisoner at Culm, by the Russian General Osterman. Was marched within twenty leagues of Siberia, and was treated by the Russians with ungenerous severity. In 1814 he returned to France. Napoleon on his landing, gave him the command of the 2nd division. His troops were in the actual pursuit of the enemy, when he learnt the defeat of Napoleon at Waterloo. He retired to Ghent, but afterwards resided on his estate at Cassel. He died in 1830.

MACDONALD.

MACDONALD, Etienne Jaques Joseph Alexander, marshal and peer of France, duke of Tarentum, Minister of State, and grand chancellor of the legion of honor, was born at Sancerre, in France, Nov. 17, 1765, and descended from a Scotch Highland family. His father fought, with twenty other Macdonalds, at Culloden, in 1745, for the Pretender. Charles Edward, kept him concealed for many weeks, and afterwards went to France. The young Macdonald entered the French service in 1784, and was attached to the legion of the lieutenant general, count Maillebois, which was sent to Holland to support the opponents of the hereditary Landholder. He embraced the principles of the revolution, rose rapidly to the rank of brigadier general, in the war of 1792, and served with distinction in 1794 under Pichegru, in the army of the North, in Holland and East Friesland. In 1796, he commanded at Dusseldorf and Cologne, as general of Division; soon after joined the army of the Rhine, and at length of Italy, under Bonaparte, where he established his military reputation. After the peace of Campo-Formio, he was in the army under Berthier, which took possession of Rome and the states of the Church, and as governor of the latter he declared Rome a republic. But Mack advanced to Rome with 50,000 men, and Macdonald was forced to fall back with his troops to the army of the French Commander in-Chief, Championnet. The latter was soon strong enough to venture an attack, and Macdonald contributed essentially to the victories at Trento, Monterosi, Baccano, Calvi, and Civita Castellana. Dec. 14 he marched into Rome the second time. After the removal of Championnet, in the spring of 1799, he was made general of the French army of Naples. While he was here carrying on war against Cardinal Ruffo, and the Calabrians, Suwaroff and Melas had conquered Lombardy and had advanced to Turin. By skilful marches, Moreau defended the frontiers of France, and the passes to Genoa. He then advanced to form a junction with Macdonald, who had evacuated Lower Italy. But instead of pursuing his march, came by to Genoa. Macdonald, ambitious to defeat the enemy alone, marched through Modena, Parma and Piacenza, the road to Voghera. He, indeed, drove the Austrians under Hohenzollern, from their position at Modena, June 12, 1799;

but Suwaroff and Melas pursued him over Tidone, June 17, at Trebia, not far from Piacenza, and on the 18th and 19th totally defeated his army, exhausted with long marches and bloody actions. Macdonald was wounded and obliged to return to Tuscany, with his army reduced to 22,000 men. Moreau now restrained the conqueror from further pursuit, and Macdonald succeeded in ascending the Appenines and forcing his way along the coast to Genoa to Moreau. Soon after he went to Paris and co-operated in the revolution of the 18th Brumaire. Dec. 1, 1800, he conducted the corps of reserve over the Spluger into the Grisons, and entered the Valteline. After the peace of Luneville, he was for a time French Ambassador in Denmark, from whence he returned in 1803, and received the title of the Grand Officer of the Legion of honor. His zeal in defending Moreau prevented him from being made marshal of the Empire, amongst the generals on whom this office was first conferred, in 1804. In the campaign of 1809 he passed the Piave with the right wing of the Viceroy, took Laybach, and decided the victory of Wagram. In recompense for his services, in that action, the Emperor created him marshal of the field, adding, "I am principally indebted to you and my artillery guards for this victory." In 1810 he took the command of Augereau's division in Catalonia, and maintained his fame as a general both here and in the war against Russia, in 1812. The capitulation of the Prussians, under York, who belonged to his army, forced him to retreat upon Koenigsberg, Jan. 3, in 1813. In May, 1813, he took Merseburg, and was present in the battles of Lutzen and Bautzen, and was defeated by Blucher on the Katzbach, At Leipsic, Oct. 18 he commanded the 11th division. He also distinguished himself at Hanau, and in the bloody campaign between the Marne and the Seine. At the time of Napoleon's catastrophe, in 1814, he had several audiences with the Emperor Alexander, in favor of the Emperor. Macdonald was the first to advise abdication after which he sent in his adherance to Louis XVIII. During the hundred days he resided on his estates. After Napoleon's final overthrow he was made chancellor of the legion of honor, and was directed to disband the army of the Loire. He has distinguished himself in the chamber of peers, not less by the justness and liberalities of his sentiments than by his fidelity to the king and to the constitution. In 1825 he attended Charles X to the coronation at

Rheims, and afterwards visited England, Scotland and Ireland. After the revolution of July lived in retirement from public affairs, till his death, which took place on the 25th of September, 1840, at his chateau of Courcelles in the neighborbood of Guise.

MONCEY.

MONCEY, Bon Adrien Jeanot, Duc de Conegliano, was the son of an advocate, and was born in 1754, at Moncey, the village near Besancon. In 1874 his relatives yielding to his passion for a soldier's life, allowed him to enrol in the gendarmery of Luneville. He became captain in 1791. In 1794 we find him as general-in-chief, defeating the Spaniards at Villa Nova. Chancing to be at Paris at the revolution of 18th Brumaire, he zealously supported Napoleon, and thus opened a path to future preferment. He was appointed by the first consul inspector general of the gendarmery and in 1804 was rewarded with a marshal's baton, the title of the Duc de Conegliano, and the rank of the grand officer of the Legion of Honor. In 1802 he commanded in the Spanish province of Catalonia, but was recalled by Bonaparte to the command of the gendarmery. In 1812 he received the additional appointment of Commander-in-Chief of the Parisian National Guard, and was entrusted with the protection of the city during the Russian campaign of Napoleon. No one was more active during the defence of the capital in 1814. He organized the National Guard of Paris, and was one among the last to lay down arms after the capitulation of the city. At the beginning of the hundred days, his submission was tendered to the Bourbons, but was withdrawn as soon as Napoleon landed from Elba. He was nominated president of the commission for the trial of Marshal Ney in 1815, yet, rather than accept this nomination, he chose to be deprived of all his titles and to lie for three months in the Prison of Ham. In 1816 he was restored to his dignities, and was received also into the favor of the King. On the outbreak of the Spanish war in 1823, Moncey was far advanced in age, he accepted, however, the command of a division, and served in Catalonia with all the force and vigor of his prime. He died in April 1842.

GROUCHY.

ROUCHY, Emanuel, count, was born at Paris, 1766, entered the military service at 14 and in 1785 was appointed an officer in the King's body guard. On the breaking out of the revolution, he showed his attachment to liberal principles, left the guard in consequence, and served in the campaign of 1792 as commander of a regiment of dragoons. In the succeeding winter, he was placed at the head of the cavalry of the army of the Alps, and contributed essentially to the conquest of Savoy. He was then sent into Vendee where he distinguished himself on several occasions, but was obliged to leave the army in consequence of the decree of the convention excluding all nobles from any military command. In 1794 he was again sent into Vendee, with the rank of general of division, disappointed the attempts of the Emigrants at Quiberon, and co-operated vigorously with the measures of the general Hoche. In 1797 he was appointed second in the command of the army destined for the invasion of Ireland. A storm dispersed the fleet and he arrived in the Bay of Bantry, with a small part of the land forces and a few ships. He determined, nevertheless, to land his forces; but the Rear-Admiral Bouvet, refused to comply and Grouchy was obliged to return to France without effecting anything. In 1798 he was ordered to join the army of Italy, and received the command of the citadel of Turin, and afterwards of all Piedmont, where he distinguished himself by his prudence, moderation, and firmness. In the following year his services contributed essentially to Moreau's victories in Germany, and the battle of Hohenlinden was gained chiefly by his energy and courage. During the trial of General Moreau, he manifested his sentiments in his favor in such a manner as to incur the displeasure of Napoleon, who continued indeed to employ him in the most dangerous and important enterprizes, without rewarding his services. In the campaign against Prussia, in 1806, and 1807, he commanded a cavalry corps, compelled the corps of prince Hohenhole to capitulate at Prenzlau, and that of Blucher near Lucbeck, and distinguished himself at Friedland. From 1808 to the time of the Austrian war, he was governor of Madrid, was then attached to the army of Italy, penetrated to Hungary and distinguished himself at the battle of

Wagram. In reward for these important services he was created commander of iron crown, colonel general in the chasseurs, and grand officer of the Empire. During the campaign in Russia (1812) general Grouchy commanded one of the three cavalry corps of the grand army, took an important part in all the great operations, covered the retreat to Smolensk, and received the command of the *sacred squadroon*, composed of generals and officers, which Napoleon had organized for the security of his person, in case of extremity. Offended by the refusal of the Emperor to confide to him the command of a division of Infantry, Grouchy retired from the service. But after the battle of Leipsic, and the disastrous retreat of the French from Germany, he offered to resume his post. Napoleon, while he permitted him to choose between the army of Piedmont and the cavalry, gave him to understand that he considered that he would be most useful at the head of the cavalry, the command of which Grouchy, therefore, determined to accept. His brilliant services in the campaign of 1814, were rewarded with the baton of marshal. After the restoration he received no appointment and he therefore joined Napoleon at his return from Elba. In 1815, he received the command of the reserve cavalry of the grand army, 80 squadroons. On the 17th of June he was detatched in pursuit of the Prussians, and on the 18th, the day of the battle of Waterloo, was before Wavre. Napoleon accuses him of being the author of the defeat at Waterloo, by permitting two divisions of the Prussian army, under Blucher, to join the English forces. After the abdication of the Emperor, marshal Grouchy proclaimed Napoleon II. He was one of the 19 general officers whose arrest was ordered by the ordinance of July 24, 1815, in consequence of which he retired to the United States, where he remained until he received permission to return to France. In his observations on the campaign of 1815 published at Philadelphia, Grouchy has defended himself from the charges of the Emperor.

LEFEBVRE.

LEFEBVRE, Francois, Joseph, duke of Dantzic, marshal and peer of France, &c., born at Rufac, Upper Rhine, in 1755, after having served with distinction in the war of the Republic and the Empire, died in 1820. Having warmly embraced the new principles and distinguished himself by his prudence and firmness his promotion was rapid. In 1794 he was made general of division, and in the succeeding campaigns, continued to render himself conspicuous by his courage and military skill. He espoused the cause of General Bonaparte, whose designs he was able to forward on the 18th Brumaire, as he had, at that time, the command of the 7th military division, which included Paris. His services on the occasion were rewarded by the dignities of Senator, marshal of the Empire and the grand cross of the legion of honor. He bore an important part in the victory of Jena, distinguished himself at Eylau and received the chief command at the siege of Dantzic, at which he gave the most brilliant proofs of genius and humanity. In 1808 he served in Spain; in 1809, again in Germany, and in the Prussian campaign commanded the imperial guard. After the abdication of the Emperor, the King created him peer, and during the hundred days Napoleon included him in his upper chamber. His name was consequently erazed, after the second restoration; but in 1819 he was again summoned to take a seat. He died in Paris, Sept. 14, 1820.

MOREAU.

MOREAU, Jean Victor, one of the oldest and most celebrated generals of the French Republic, was born at Morlaix in Bretagne, in 1763. His father, destined him for the law; but led, by his decided predilection for the military profession, he fled from his studies, and enlisted in a regiment, before he had attained his 18th year. He was not, however, allowed to indulge his ruling passion, but was obliged to apply himself anew to the study of law, at Rennes, of which school he became a provost. When the revolution broke out, he had acquired considerable reputation, and in 1789 a general Confederacy of the Bretons being formed at Poictiers, he was chosen its president, and also became commander of the first battalion of volunteers, raised in the department of Morbihan, at the head of which he joined the army of the north. He subsequently favored the party of Gironde, the fall of which much affected him, and it was with great repugnance that he accepted the constitution of 1793, when finally presented to the army. In the meantime he much distinguished himself at the head of his battalion, and Pichegru, under whom he served, did all he could to befriend him. The same year he was made general of brigade, and in 1794, general of division, and was entrusted with a separate force to act in maratime Flanders, where he took many towns. He also had a share in the memorable winter campaign of 1794, in which he commanded the right wing of Pichegru's army. He was soon after named Commander-in-Chief of the army of the Rhine, and commenced that course of arduous operations which ended in the celebrated retreat, from the extremity of Germany to the French frontier, in the face of a superior army, by which his skill as a consummate tactician was so much exalted. Meantime the Republic was torn with intestine divisions, and a conspiracy was entered into by Pichegru, which it was the fortune of Moreau to discover, by a correspondence which accidently fell into his possession. After struggling for some time with his friendship for his old commander, he finally gave up the documents to the directory; but the evident reluctance with which he took this step excited suspicions at Paris and finding that he could not explain himself satisfactorily, he begged leave to retire, which was granted. His talents, as a general, again brought him forward, and in 1798 he was sent to command the army of Italy, where, after some brilliant successes, he was obliged to give way to Russian force under Suwarrow, and he managed another retreat with great skill. On quitting the command in Italy for that on the Rhine, he visited Paris, where he received some propositions to strengthen the party of the declining directory, to which he could not accede. On the return of Bonaparte from Egypt, he at first cordially supported him; but a coldness and jealousy ensued notwithstanding which the latter, as the first consul, entrusted him with the command of the armies of the Danube and the Rhine. The passage of these rivers, with the battle of Moskirch, Engen, Memmingen, Biberach, Hochstadt, Noerdlingen, and others, followed, ending with the decisive victory of Hohenlinden, which induced the Austrians to ask for peace. On his return to Paris, he was received by the first consul, with the most flattering attention; and he soon after contracted an alliance with a young lady of birth and fortune, whose ambition with that of her connections, is supposed to have fomented the discontent which soon after induced him to retire to his Estate at Grosbois. He was finally accused of participation in the conspiracy of Pichegru and Georges, was brought to trial with 54 other persons, declared guilty upon slight evidence, and sentenced to two years imprisonment, and to bear the expenses of the suit. He was, however, allowed to travel, in lieu of imprisonment, and to seek assylum in the U. S. of America, on condition that he would not return to France without permission from the government. He accordingly embarked at Cadiz in 1805, and safely reached America, where he bought a fine Estate near Morrisville, on the Delaware. Here he remained some years in peace, until listening to the invitation of allies, and especially of Russia, he embarked for Europe in the July of that year, and reaching Gottenburg, he proceeded to Prague. Here he found the Emperor of Austria and Russia, with the King of Prussia all of whom received him with great cordiality, and he was induced to aid in the direction of the allied armies against his own country. It was a fatal resolution to himself; for on the 27th of August, soon after his arrival, while conversing with the Emperor Alexander on horse back, in the battle before Dresden, a cannon ball fractured his right knee and leg and carried away the calf of the left so as render the amputation of both necessary. After languishing for five days he expired Sept. 1st, 1813. He was burried at St. Petersburg, and the Emperor of Russia made an ample provision for his widow, who also received the title of *Marechale*, from Louis XVIII. The manners of Moreau were simple, and he was humane and generous as well as brave. His great merits as a soldier, all parties admit; but much of his personal conduct as a partisan, and especially that which led to the termination of his life will be judged of variously by persons of different political opinions.

KLEBER.

KLEBER, Jean Baptiste, a French general, distinguished not less for his humanity and integrity than for his courage, activity and coolness, was one of the ablest soldiers, which the revolution, so fertile in military genius, produced. Young Kleber was peacefully occupied as an architect, when the revolutionary troubles led him to the career of arms. He was born at Strasburg in 1755, and had received some education in the military academy at Munich, through the agency of some German gentlemen to whom he rendered a service. From 1776 to 1783, he had served in the Austrian army, against the Turks. Having entered a French volunteer corps, as a simple grenadier, in 1792, his talents soon procured him notice, and after the capture of Mayence he was made general of brigade. Although he openly expressed his horror at the atrocious policy of the revolutionary government, his services were too valuable to be lost, and he distinguished himself as a general of division, in the campaign of 1795 and 1796. In 1797, Kleber, dissatisfied with the directory, retired from the service; but General Bonaparte prevailed upon him to join the expedition to Egypt. Although no favorite of the General-in-Chief, yet such were his talents that he displayed in the campaign in Syria, and the battle of Aboukir, and such was the esteem in which he was held by the army, that Bonaparte left him the command when he himself returned to France. His situation was difficult; the army was weakened by a series of laborious marches, and sanguinary conflicts, and all communication with France was intercepted; yet he maintained himself successfully against the enemy, and introduced order into the government, but in the midst of new preparations for securing possession of the country, he was assassinated by a Turkish fanatic, June 14, 1800.

DESAIX.

DESAIX, de Voygoux, Louis Charles, Antoine, a French general, born 1768, at St. Hilaire d' Ayat, of a noble family. He served in 1794, in the Northern army of the Rhine, under Moreau, in 1796, he defended the bridge of Khel, in November of that year. In 1797, he accompanied Bonaparte to Egypt, contributed to his first victory and was thence sent to the conquest of the Upper Egypt, where Murad Bey, notwithstanding his defeat, necessarily harrassed his conqueror. Bonaparte soon returned to Europe, as did Desaix himself, after the treaty of El Arish, concluded with the Turks and English. On his arrival in France he learned that Bonaparte had departed for Italy, hastened to join him and took command of the reserve. A third part of the French army were already disabled when Desaix arrived, (June

14, 1800,) on the field of Marengo. He immediately advanced to the charge, but fell, mortally wounded, by a cannon ball, just as the victory declared for the French. A monument was erected to him on the St. Bernard, also on the plains of Marengo, where he fell. Desaix was as just and disinterested as he was brave. The inhabitants of Cairo gave him the title of the *Just Sultan*.

MASSENA.

MASSENA, Andre, duke of Rivoli and Prince of Esslingen, marshal of France, &c., was born in 1758, at Nice, and rose from a common soldier to the rank of commander. At the commencement of the French revolution he was an inferior officer in the Sardinian troops; but in 1729, when the warriors of the new republic had ascended mount Cenis, he joined their ranks, soon distinguished himself by his sagacity and courage, and was made a commissioned officer, and in 1793 general of brigade. Here he learned without a master, the science of war, in the skirmishes. In April, 1794, he was appointed general of division, and took command of the right wing of the Italian army. He was the constant companion in arms of Bonaparte, who, after successful battle of Roveredo (1796) against Beaulieu, called him the favorite child of victory. The commander in chief sent him to Vienna, to conclude negotiations for peace, and in 1796, to Paris, to procure the ratification of the treaty. While Bonaparte was in Egypt, Massena and Moreau were the hopes of France. In 1799 Massena displayed his ability as commander-in-chief in Switzerland. After having ended the war successfully he was forced to fall back to the Albis, on account of the ill fortune of Jourdan on the Danube. Here he took a strong position, watching his opportunity, and by the battle of Zurich, September 25, prevented the junction of Korsakoff and Suwaroff, who had already ascended mount St. Gothard. This battle, the first that the Russians had lost in the open field for a century, decided the separation of Russia from Austria, and saved France. After Massena had reconquered the Helvetian and Rhaecian Alps, he was sent to Italy to check the victorious career of the Austrians. He hastened with the small force, which could be assembled, to the support of Genoa, his defence of which is among his most remarkable achievements. Ten days before the battle of Marengo, when all his resources were exhausted, Massena obtained an honorable capitulation. The consul

Bonaparte, who now returned to Paris, gave him the chief command of the army. Peace soon followed. Massena was chosen member of the *corps legislatif* by the department of the Seine, and in 1804 was created marshal of the Empire. In 1805 he received the chief command in Italy. After the peace of Pressburg, Massena was sent by Napoleon to take possession of the kingdom of Naples for Joseph, and captured Gaeta. After the battle of Eylau, in 1807, Napoleon summoned him to Poland, to take the command of the right wing of the French army. After the peace of Tilsit, war having broken out in Spain, Massena took the field with the title of duke of Rivoli; but in 1809 he was recalled to Germany. He was present in the battles of Eckmuhl, Ratisbon, Ebersberg, Esslingen, and Wagram. At Esslingen, his constancy and firmness saved the French army from total destruction, and Napoleon rewarded him with the dignity of prince of Esslingen. After the peace, he hastened to Spain, to deliver Portugal from the hands of the British. Wellington, retired before him and took a strong position at Torres Vedras for the defense of Lisbon, till want of provisions made it impossible for the French forces to hold out longer. Massena was at last obliged to retire, Napoleon recalled him from Spain, and, in 1812, left him without a command. In 1814 he commanded at Toulon, declared for Louis XVIII, and was created commander of the order of St Louis. At the landing of Napoleon, in 1815, his conduct in Toulon was by no means doubtful. When the Emperor was reestablished, he swore allegiance to him, and was made peer, and commander of the national guard at Paris, and contributed much to the preservation of tranquility of the city during the turbulent period which preceeded the return of the King. He lived afterwards in retirement, and his death was hastened by chargin at the conduct of the royalists. He died April 4th, 1817.

LANNES.

LANNES, John, marshal of France, duke of Montebello, was born in 1769, was apprentice to a dyer, and in 1792, on the invasion of French soil, entered the army as Sergeant Major. His talents and services had raised him to the rank of *chef de brigade,* as early as 1795, and General Bonaparte created him Colonel after the battle of Millesimo. After distinguishing himself in Italy and Egypt, whence he returned with Bonaparte, and serving under the first consul in Italy, he was made marshal of the Empire in 1804, and subsequently the duke of Montebello. In the campaign against Austria (1805), he rendered important service, and at the battle of Austerlitz commanded the left wing of the main army. At Jena, Eyl- au, Friedland (1807), at Tudelo Saragosa in Spain, Marshal Lannes obtained a brilliant renown. In the campaign of 1809, against Austria, he lost both his legs by a cannon ball in the battle of Essligen or Aspern, May 22, and died May 31. Napoleon was strongly moved at the sight of the dying Lannes, who was the favorite of the Emperor. His eldest son was created a peer by the King in 1815. He visited the United States in 1828, and during the revolution of 1830 fought on the side of the people.

PONIATOWSKI.

PONIATOWSKI descended from an illustrious Polish family— born in 1763, served with courage against the Russians in 1792, and on the accession of his uncle to the confederation of Targowitz, he left the service with most of the best officers. When the Poles attempted in 1794 to drive the Russians out of the country he again joined the Polish camp as a volunteer. Kosciuszko gave him the command of a division, at the head of which he distinguished him- self at two sieges of Warsaw. After the surrender of the city he went to Vienna, and, rejecting the offers of Catharine and Paul, lived in retirement on his return to Poland, on his estate near Warsaw. The creation of the Duchy of Warsaw rekindled the hopes of the Polish patriots, and Poniatowski accepted the place of minister of war in the new State. In 1809, he commanded the Polish army against the superior Austrian force which was sent to occupy the Duchy, com- pelled it to retire rather by skillful manouvres than by force of arms and penetrated into Galicia. In the war of 1812 against Russia he was again at the head of the Polish force and distinguished him- self in all the principal affairs of this chequered campaign. After the battle of Leipsic, during which Napoleon created him marshal of France, he was ordered October 19, to cover the retreat of the French army. The enemy were already in possession of the suburbs of Leipsic, and had thrown light troops over the Elster, when the prince arrived with a few followers, at the river, the bridge over which had been blown up by the French. Poniatowski, already wounded, plunged with his horse, into the stream, which swallowed up horse and rider. His body was first found on the 24th, and

burried with all the honors of his rank, on the 26th. It was afterwards removed to Warsaw, and in 1816, was deposited in the
cathedral at Cracow. Thorwaldsen has erected an equestrian statue
of Poniatowski, for the city of Warsaw.

SAVARY.

AVARY, Rene, duke of Rovigo, was born in 1774. He was
Napoleon's minister of police and served with distinction, in
1789 in the line, also in 1796, under Moreau, and in 1799, under
Desaix in Egypt. After Desaix's death at Marengo, in 1800 he
became Napoleon's Adjutant General, and soon after was entrusted
with the charge of the secret police. Bold, active and dexterous, as
for instance in the discovery of the conspiracy of George and
Pichegru, and at the same time zealously devoted to the Emperor, he
soon obtained the confidence of the latter. Napoleon employed him
on important missions. After the battle of Austerlitz, he was sent
to the Russian and Austrian headquarters, and in 1808, to Ferdinand
VII, at Madrid, whom he induced to come to Bayonne. On account
of a brilliant charge which he succesffully made at the head of his
regiment at the battle of Friedland in 1807, the Emperor made him
duke of Rovigo; and when Fouche fell into disgrace, he was appointed June 3, 1810 minister of police. After Napoleon's return from
Elba, Fouche was made minister of police, and Savary was appointed general superintendent of the *gens d'armes,* and a peer of
France. It is well known that the British government refused to
give him permission to accompany Napoleon to St. Helena. Having been detained as a prisoner at Malta, he escaped, in April, 1816
to Smyrna. Thence he went in 1817, to Trieste, in order to repair
to Paris, to defend himself against a sentence of death passed on
him December 25, 1816, by a court martial, but he was detained
at Gratz, until he returned to Smyrna in June 1818, where he engaged in mercantile business. In 1819 he went to London and
thence to Paris, where, December 27 of that year, he presented
himself before the court and was acquitted. He then lived retired,
but went to Berlin in 1823 to bring before the Prussian court of
justice an action against the Prussian Exchequer for indemnification
for the loss of his dotations in the Prussian dominions, which the
King presented to General Gneisenau. Failing in this object, he

went back to Paris, and, in order to refute a passage in the *memorial* of Count Las Cases, published a fragment from his memories *(Sur le Catastrophe du duc d'Enghien)*, denying his privity to the arrest and execution of the duke, and maintaining on the contrary, that the whole was planned and carried into execution without the previous knowledge of Napoleon, by the minister who was then at the head of foreign affairs (Talleyrand). But Talleyrand justified himself before Louis XVIII; and other publications connected with this affair, particularly those of General Hulin and Dupin, bear so hard on the duke of Rovigo, that it is difficult to believe him not to have been privy to the hurried execution of the sentence. The duke of Rovigo was thereupon banished from the court, and from that time lived in close retirement. He appears to be a man of courage and adroitness, but destined by nature to follow the lead of men of more decided talent and character. He was appointed governor of Algiers in 1832 and died in Paris in 1833, of a disease contracted by him from exposure to the climate of Algiers.

DUROC.

DUROC, Michael, duke of Friuli, grand marshal of the palace, senator, general of division, grand order of the legion of honor, and of nearly all the orders of Europe, was born at Pont-a Mousson in 1772. His father was of an ancient family of Auvergne, having become captain and knight of St. Louis, he married and established himself in Lorraine. Young duke was early destined for the army, and studied at the military school at Pont-a Mousson. March 1, 1792 he was made lieutenant of artillery. He then served in the republican armies. Honorable mention is made of his name in the battles of the Italian army, particularly at the siege of Mantua, and at the battle of Sismone, in 1796 he served, during the first campaign in Italy, as aid-de-camp to the general of artillery, Lespinasse. Being subsequently appointed aid-de-camp to general Bonaparte, he soon made himself conspicuous by coolness, courage and ability. He distinguished himself at the battle of Grimolano, where he was wounded, and his horse was killed under him. At the passage of the Izonso, in Friuli, he was mentioned as one of the bravest, and most able officers. The title of the duke of Friuli,

which he received, ten years afterwards, was chosen in allusion to
his conduct at I zonso. Duroc followed General Bonaparte into
Egypt, and was promoted to the rank of chief of battalion the
25th of Brumaire, year VI. During this campaign in which his
services were of the greatest value, his name was again mentioned
with honor after the battle of Salahia, the successful result of which
was mainly owing to his valor. During the expedition into Syria,
at the siege of Jaffa, Duroc seeing grenadiers falling at the post of
the breach, and wavering, put himself at their head, and engaged
hand to hand with several Turks. The army seeing him disappear
in a tower which was defended with great fury, gave him up for
lost, but soon received him with shouts on seeing him appear on the
top, master of the tower and of the ramparts. After having distinguished himself on several occasions, before St. Jean d'Acre, he
was severely wounded by the bursting of a howitzer in one of the
hot assaults made during the siege, the most bloody and obstinate
in the military annals of France. He distinguished himself no less
at the battle of Aboukir. Being made chief of brigade, he accompanied General Bonaparte on his return to France; he was almost
the only aid-de-camp of the commander in chief who survived the
expedition; four had been killed in the campaign. Duroc took part
in the events of the 18th Brumaire, and, a few days after, was sent
to the court of Berlin, where he was received with great distinction.
The Embassy contributed to preserve peace between these two
countries. War continuing between France and Austria, the first
consul set out for the campaign, which he terminated at Marengo.
His name was honorably mentioned at the passage of Ticino, where
he was the first to leap into a boat, at the head of the grenadiers.
After the peace of Amiens, he was sent, on diplomatic missions to
the courts of St. Petersburg, Stockholm and Copenhagen. On his
return, he was promoted to the rank of general of brigade and governor of the Tuillers; and on the 9th Fructidor, year X, he was
made general of division. When the first consul assumed the title
of Emperor, he made Duroc grand marshal of the palace. The
courtier and favorite never ceased to be a soldier. He accompanied
Napoleon in all his campaigns, in 1805 he was charged with the
mission to the Russian court, at the time when Napoleon was
marching against Vienna. He rejoined the army previously to the
battle of Austerlitz, and took the command of the division of grena-

diers, which had been left without a head in consequence of the wound of Oudinot. At the battle of Austerlitz he also commanded a division of this chosen corps. During the campaign of Prussia, in 1806 Duroc was commissioned to sign the treaty of peace with the King of Saxony; and at a latter period, he was the principal negotiator of the armistice which preceeded the peace of Tilsit. He followed Napoleon to Spain, and during the campaign of Wagram. At the battle of Esslingen he arranged and directed his batteries in such a way as to arrest the progress of the enemy in a decisive movement. After the battle of Znaym Napoleon sent him to the arch duke Charles to negotiate an armistice. On the return from the Russian campaign (in 1812), Duroc reorganized the imperial guard, which at this time and on several other occasions, he commanded. Before his last departure for the army, he was appointed senator. Duroc finally followed Napoleon to Germany in 1813 and was killed May 23, after the battle of Lutzen, on entering the village of Merkersdorf, by a ball, which also killed General Kirschner with whom he was conversing behind the Emperor. This ball was the last which fell on that day, and the piece from which it was discharged was at so great a distance and surrounded by so many obstacles, that it is inconceivable how it could have reached the place. Napoleon visited Duroc on his death-bed and mingled tears with his farewell. He lost in him a true councellor, a faithful friend, and one of his bravest officers. The death of the duke of Friuli and of the duke of Montebello are the two events on which Napoleon showed the greatest sensibility. Successively charged with the most important duties, military and political, the duke of Friuli was ever remarkable for a moderation wise in a soldier, for ability, disinterestedness, modesty, firmness, and a presence of mind which never deserted him. For 15 years he was friend and confidant of that extraordinary man. When Napoleon left France in 1815 and embarked on board of the Bellerophon, he wished to live in England under the name of Col. Duroc. Seven years afterwards we have another proof of the constant and affectionate rememberance which Napoleon retained of him. He left to his daughter one of the largest legacies, bequeathed by his will.

CAMBRONNE.

CAMBRONNE, Piere, Jaques Ettienne, baron, general, commander of the legion of honor, and field marshal, born December 26, 1770, at St. Sebastien, near Nantes, was descended from an opulent family and enjoyed a good education. Under the republic, and under Napoleon, he served in every campaign, and became so celebrated on account of his personal bravery, that the soldiers wished to give him the title of first grenadier of France, after the death of Latour d'Auvergne, but he declined the honor. He was made commander of the chasseurs of the imperial guard, and was at Fontainebleau when Napoleon abdicated. He went with him to the island of Elba as chief of the division of the old guard, which accompanied him into his exile. Cambronne commanded the little corps with which Napoleon landed, March 1, 1815, in the gulf of St. Juan, and signed the address to the French army summoning them to return to Napoleon's standard. On the field of battle at Waterloo, he was taken prisoner by the British, among those who were severely wounded. His celebrated answer to the British proposal of capitulation is well known. " La garde meurt, elle ne se rend pas." The guard dies but does not surrender. He was one of the 19 generals of Napoleon who by the royal decree of July 24, 1815, were to be tried by a court martial. He returned from his captivity as a prisoner of war, and appeared in person before the tribunal. As he had taken no oath to the Bourbons, he was acquitted. The sentence was revised, and the acquittal confirmed. In 1820 he was appointed by Louis XVIII to be commandant of the fortress of Lille, with the rank of a " marshal de camp" which office, he however resigned in 1824, on account of the shattered condition of his health. He died March 5th 1826.

EUGENE BEAUHARNAIS.

EUGENE BEAUHARNAIS, duke of Leuchtenberg, prince of Eichstad, ex-viceroy of Italy, was born September 3, 1781. He was the son of the viscount Alexander Beauharnais, who was guilotined 1794, and Josephine Tascher de la Pagerie, afterwards wife of Napoleon and Empress of France. During the French revolution, Eugene entered the military service, and at the age of

12 years, accompanied his father when he took the command of the army of the Rhine. After his father's death, he joined Hoche, in La Vendee, when his mother was in prison. After the 9th Thermidor, he returned to his mother in Paris, and remained three years devoted to study. In 1796, Josephine was married to General Bonaparte. then commander in chief of the army in Italy, and Eugene accompanied his father-in-law in his campaigns in Italy and in Egypt. He was promoted to a high rank in the service, and in 1805, created a prince of France and viceroy of Italy. In the same year, he distinguished himself in the campaign against Austria, and after the peace of January 13, 1806, married the princes Augusta of Bavaria. In 1807 Napoleon made him Prince of Venice, and declared him his heir to the kingdom of Italy. He administered the government of Italy with great prudence and moderation, and was much beloved by his subjects. In the war of 1809, he was at first unsuccessful against the arch duke John, but soon afterwards gained the battle of Raab, and distinguished himself at Wagram. He conducted with great prudence on the occasion of the divorce of Napoleon from his mother. The 3d of March 1810, Napoleon appointed him successor of the prince primate, who had been created grand duke of Frankfort. In the Russian campaign he commanded the third corps d'armee and distinguished himself in the battle of Ostrowno, Mohilew, and that of the Moskwa (Borodino). In the disastrous retreat, he did not desert the wrecks of his division for a moment, but shared its trials and dangers with the soldiers and encouraged them by his example. To him and to Ney, France was indebted for the preservation of the remains of the army during that fatal retreat. On the departure of Napoleon and Murat, he was left in the chief command, and showed great talent at that dangerous conjuncture. We find him again at the battle of Lutzen, of May 2, 1813, where by surrounding the right wing of the enemy, he decided the fate of the day. Napoleon sent him from Dresden to the defence of Italy, now menaced by the enemy's forces, where military operations commenced after the dissolution of the congress of Prague, and the accession of Austria to the league of the allied powers. Eugene maintained the defence of Italy, even after the desertion of Murat. After the fall of Napoleon, he conducted an armistice with count Bellegarde, by which he delivered Lombardy

and all upper Italy, to the Austrians. Eugene then went immediately to Paris, and then to his father-in-law, at Munich. He was at the congress of Vienna. On the return of Napoleon from Elba, he was obliged to leave Vienna and retire to Baireuth. He was an inactive spectator of the events of 1815. By the articles of Fontainebleau, an indemnification was assigned him for the loss of his estates in Italy, which were valued at 20 to 25 millions of francs, but the congress of Vienna confirmed his dotation in the ward of Ancona, and the King of Naples was obliged to pay him 5 million francs. By an ordinance of the King of Bavaria, he was created duke of Leuchtenberg, November 1817. The Bavarian Principality of Eichstad was bestowed upon him, and his posterity declared capable of inheriting in case of a failure of the Bavarian line. He died at Munich February 21, 1824, leaving two sons and four daughters. Prince Eugene, under a simple exterior, concealed a noble character and great talents. Honor, integrity, humanity, and love of order and justice, were the principal traits of his character. Wise in the counsel, undaunted in the field, and moderate in the exercise of power, he never appeared greater than in the midst of reverses, as the events of 1813 and 1814 prove. He was inaccessible to the spirit of party, benevolent and beneficent, and more devoted to the good of others than to his own. He died of an organic disorder of the brain.

NAPOLEON.

NAPOLEON BONAPARTE. This extraordinary genius was born Aug 15th, 1769, at Ajaccio in the island of Corsica, and was the second son of Charles Bonaparte, a Corsican nobleman, and Lettitia, his wife, whose maiden name was Rumolini. He received a place in the royal military school at Brienne in 1779, where he remained until 1784. During his stay there, his conduct is represented as having been unexceptionable. In 1786 he commenced his military life, being appointed in that year a second lieutenant in the regiment of artillery La Fere. When he was twenty years old the French revolution removed barriers to his great career. In 1793 he was appointed captain. In 1794 when Mountain party developed its energies, and finding no foundation for rational liberty on the first emersion of the country from the corruption and tyrany of centuries, strove to save it by terrorism. Terror was to silence its adversaries, glory to unite its friends. Foreign enemies also contributed to develope the powers of France. Fourteen armies were raised, and the victorious legions of Rome became the exemplars of the republican warriors, who thirsted for glory and vengeance. Such a state of things would naturally awake a strong excitement in young Bonaparte, a soldier, whose age and profession would alone make him eager for distinction. Lyons was destroyed and 4000 inhabitants had been shot, and treachery opened the gates of Toulon. Bonaparte received the command of artillery there and Toulon was taken. The English before evacuating the place set fire to the town as well as to the French ships. It is probable that the enmity which Bonaparte manifested against the English during all the period of his power, was in some measure owing to the impression made upon him by their conduct at Toulon. December 19th, the day of taking Toulon, the commissioners appointed him general of brigade and commander of artillery of the army of Italy. The 9th Thermidor (27 July), overthrew the reign of the Terrosists and General Bonaparte was arrested by order of Sallicctti and Albitti, because younger Robespierre and Ricord, who were proscribed on the occasion of this revolution had placed the greatest confidence in the young officer. A guard was stationed at his door, and his papers seized, but in a fortnight he was set at liberty and restored to his command. He next served under General Dumerbion in Piedmont, who, after the battle of Cairo (in Piedmont), acknowledged in a letter to the commisioners, that he owed to the young officer the skilful combinations which had secured the victory. The cast which political notions of Bonaparte received from the stormy character of the period is apparent in most of his future conduct— About this time he became acquainted with Josephine, whom he met at the house of Barras, and March 19, 1796, was married to her. He was then appointed as general in chief of the army destined for Italy. His brilliant career commenced when he was but 27 years old. The coalition at that time existing against France was formidable; it was composed of England, Austria, Piedmont, Naples, Bavaria and all the minor states of Germany and Italy, but France really made war against Austria, which it was determined to attack chiefly in Italy. The conduct of this war was entrusted to Bonaparte. Arrived at Nice, his headquarters, the young general had first to obtain an influence with veteran officers, already distinguished by a series of successes. Augereau, Massena, La Harpe, &c. The position of the French army in the rocks of Liguria was dangerous, Bonaparte saw that nothing could save them but victories. His proclamation to his soldiers, admirably calculated to excite their enthusiasm, pride, and feeling of honor had a striking effect, and like Frederick the Great, he astonished his enemies by a new system of tactics. Within six days, in which victory followed victory, he separated the Piedmontese from Austrian armies, reduced 12,000 Austrians to inactivity, took forty cannons, became master of the fortress by Coni, Ceva, Tortona and Alexander, and obliged the King of Sardinia to sue for peace. The eyes of all Europe were now turned upon the young general, and the officers of the hostile armies themselves acknowledged the superiority of his system of concentration. Massena, Augereau and Joubert distinguished themselves in this campaign; but the superiority of Bonaparte was so decided that jealousy was silent, and his soldiers begun to adore him. The celebrated battle of Lodi, where Bonaparte's personal courage was conspicuous, was fought on the 10th of May (1796). Then came many military exploits and diplomatic master strokes that have shed a lustre on Napoleon's name. The battle of Arcola was fought October 15th, and it was here that he raised a standard in the midst of a murderous fire, took the lead, his aid-de-camp Muiron was killed upon his body. He was so successful in arms and diplomacy that the trembling directory wished to get rid of him, he was accordingly appointed to the command of the "army of England" which, however, was intended for Egypt A fleet was very speedily collected, with more than 30,000 chosen troops and set sail May 19th (1798). The capture of Malta (June 12), and of Alexandria (July 2), were the first results of the expedition. The victory over the Turks (July 25, 1799) and the recovery of Aboukir (August 2), were Bonaparte's last achievements in Egypt His brother Joseph informed him of the critical state of the republic and leaving the command of the army in the hands of Kleber he returned to France. Well might Bonaparte make it a matter of reproach to the directory, that he had left the republic victorious and powerful and found it vanquished and feeble. The demand for a change of government was universal. He swore fidelity to the republic and on the 9th of November (1799), overthrew the directorial government. The grenadiers entered the hall at the command of Bonaparte, but stopped a moment, while a member of the council (General Jourdan), warned them that they were guilty of a violation of the rights of the representatives of the people. They then advanced, with fixed bayonets and drove the council from the hall, General Leclerc, their commander, crying out, "In the name of General Bonaparte, the legislative council is dissolved, grenadiers forward." Thus ended the constitution of 1795. Bonaparte was appointed consul for ten years with powers such as few constitutional Kings possess. With him were joined two consuls, with comparatively little power. Several conspiracies were soon discovered for the assassination of the first consul but every one of them failed. As soon as General Bonaparte seized the reins of government, he directed his attention to the formation and completion of the code of laws. An interesting period, military and diplomatic in the French history then follows, when on October 9th France seemed to be at peace with its adversaries. The celebration of the general peace at Paris November 9th, was splendid, and the people gave Bonaparte the title of *pacificator*. The peace of Amiens was concluded, with England, March 26, 1802. The celebration of this peace was solemnized April 28, in Notre Dame; from which event we may date, the reestablishment of the Catholic worship. A law of amnesty, which granted the emigrants permission to return, was now passed, also a law establishing the Legion of Honor. Napoleon was obliged to concentrate the whole government in himself for the better carrying out of his plans through all the ramifications of the social system. Civil liberty, it must be acknowledged, is the great aim of modern civilization, and has never begun with the military glory of victorious legions, but if the growth of the military spirit was necessary, that is to say, if Napoleon could not prevent it in the existing circumstances in order to secure the ends of justice, property and person, then, if this necessity is to be deplored, the individual should not be condemned. After the military spirit had been inflamed to the highest pitch and the military establishment had acquired a gigantic extent; after the government had become absolute, and the ambition of Napoleon, the last infirmity of the noble minds, had received so much excitement—that he then, and especially towards the end of his reign, mistook sometimes the means for the end, cannot be denied. After the concordate with the pope was concluded and the Catholic worship was reestablished—then came the question "Shall Napoleon Bonaparte be consul for life." It was answered in the affirmative, unanimously by the whole nation, and he reserved the right of nominating his successor. The troubles with England begun to increase, the non-adherence to the treaty of Amiens was complained of, and March 13, 1803, Bonaparte announced in a solemn audience of foreign ministers the approaching rupture with England, it eventually resulted in the "Continental system," which Napoleon considered the only way to force England into a lasting peace with France. It was the most gigantic political project ever attempted, to obtain which many wars were waged and thrones overturned and established, and which finally brought ruin to the contriver. June 20th, 1803 the continental system went into operation. A conspiracy was soon discovered, February 15, 1804, against the life and government of the first consul, the heads of which were Pichegru and George Cadoudal. This and other attempts against the favorite of the nation brought the question of the hereditary power in France. On the 18th of May Cambaceres addressed him for the first time, *sire* and *your majesty.* The dignity of the marshal of the Empire was conferred on Berthier, Murat, Moncey, Jourdan, Massena, Augereau, Bernadotte, Soult, Brune, Lannes, Mortier, Ney, Davoust, &c. Seven days later, the Emperor received the oath of fidelity, from the senate, the tribunate, and the legislative body. Here follows an interesting period about which we refer the reader to the history of France. In the beginning of 1805, Napoleon wrote with his own hand, a letter to George III, offering to conclude peace for the welfare of Europe, but lord Mulgrave, then Secretary of State answered to the French minister of foreign affairs, that the King could not accept the proffer without consulting his allies. Napoleon, may now have first determined to banish all regard for the balance of power for England, and to adopt a federative system, in which France should have a preponderating influence. May 26, he crowned himself with the iron crown in the cathedral at Milan, pronouncing these words, whilst he took the crown from the altar: *Dieu me la donne; gare a qui la touche* (God has given it to me, woe to him who touches it). Before he left Italy, the convents were abolished, with the exception of the charitable orders, and those which devoted themselves to instruction. Notwithstanding the benefits which his policy conferred on the country, these changes were considered as violations of the law of nations, and incorporation of Genoa with the Empire became the pretext for a war long resolved upon. April 11, 1805, a treaty was concluded between Russia and England, by which they engaged to use most effective means to form a general coalition against France. An army of 500,000 men was to force this Empire to restore the balance of power in Europe. The plan of this campaign is a striking exhibition of Napoleon's genius, and the sagacity with which he made his victories conduce to his political objects, shows his great qualifications for ruling. September 25 and 26 his army crossed the Rhine. October 2 he concluded a treaty of Ludwigsburg, with the elector of Wirtemberg, which gave him a new accession of troops; on the same day Bavarians formed a junction with the French army. On the 3d Bernadotte marched with his corps through the neutral Prussian possessions in Franconia. Thus on the 4th, the Austrians were menaced on the flank and rear. On the 8th, Murat gained an important victory at Wertingen. On the 10th, Napoleon concluded a treaty with Baden at Esslingen. On the 14th, the Austrians were partially defeated at Ulm; and on the next day another Austrian corps at Trochtelfingen and another at Bopfingen; Napoleon's fortune seemed, nevertheless to waver. On the 21st, the French and Spanish fleet was annihilated by Nelson at Trafalgar; the arch duke Charles entered Italy; Prussia put its troops in. motion, the Russian Emperor appeared himself in Berlin, and persuaded Frederick William to take part in the war; but the French advanced without delay into Austria, and November 13th, Murat entered Vienna, and Napoleon Schonbrunn. The battle of Austerlitz was fought on the 2d of December, after which followed the peace of Pressburg; the rapid series of decisive victories which followed, was almost unexampled. A decree of the senate conferred on the Emperor the title of Great. Pitt, his implacable enemy, had died, January 23, 1806. In July, the confederacy of the Rhine was formed in Paris, and Napoleon, as its protector, became the ruler of the greater part of Germany. The battles of Auerstadt and Jena were fought Octocer 14th. November 21 Napoleon issued the famous decree, declaring Great Britian in a state of blockade, and strictly prohibiting all intercourse with her. The French armies continued to advance. At Posen Napoleon promised to the long wronged Poles the restoration of their kingdom. A Russian army hastened, indeed, to aid the King of Prussia, but the battle of Pultusk, December 26, the bloody battle of Eylau, February 7 and 8, the capitulation of Dantzic, and the battle of Friedland, finally resulted in a peace between Russia and France 7th of July, and on the 9th between France and Prussia at Tilsit. The interview of Napoleon and Alexander at Tilsit resulted in a personal friendship of the two monarchs. England suspected the conclusion of secret articles of peace between them, and insisted on knowing them. As this was refused, she feared that Denmark, unable to maintain her neutrality in such a state of things, would yield up her ships to supply French loss at Trafalgar. The English cabinet, therefore, resolved to possess themselves of the Danish fleet, and succeeded September 7th, after the bombardment of Copenhagen. The Danish fleet consisted of 18 vessels of the line, 15 frigates, 6 brigs and 25 gun-boats. The fate of Denmark, at this time, was the harder, as she had honestly struggled to preserve neutrality, but in great political crises, it is impossible either for nations or for individuals to remain neutral. Still further to straighten England, Napoleon now shut up the ports of the Pyrenean peninsula. Portugal which has for the last century, always been dependent on England attracted especially Napoleon's attention. Spain, ever since 1795 subservient to France, had been so merely from fear; and when Napoleon, in 1806, was occupied with Russia, Godoy the prince of peace, had issued a proclamation calling upon the Spaniards to take up arms against the common enemy. Pradt, ascribes Napoleon's conduct towards Spain, to his being irritated by this foolish proclamation, but the plans of Napoleon were not likely to be influenced by the proclamation of a subject like Godoy. Napoleon had also informed the prince regent of Portugal in August, that he must give up all connection with England, confiscate English merchandize in Portuguese ports, and adhere without reserve to the continental system, if the house of Braganza wished to remain on the throne—a demand which it was actually impossible to fulfil, besides being inconsistent with the oath taken by every ruler of Portugal. When a French army approached, he and his family embarked, Nov. 29th, for Brazil, the next day, Junot entered Lisbon, and the conquest of Portugal was completed. The political state of Spain at this time was deplorable, and the condition of the Spanish court shocking. It consisted of an imbecile King—a Queen who did not even seem to observe appearances, an ambitious and intriguing favorite and prime minister; and, an heir-apparent conspiring against his father's throne. On the 19th of October Napoleon set out for Spain, where his presence brought victory to the French arms. But the threatening movements of the Austrian cabinet speedily obliged him to return. Austria declared war April 9, 1809. Napoleon entered Ingolstast on the 18th. On the 20th he defeated the Austrians at Abensberg; on the 21st at Landshut; on the 22d at Eckmuhl, on the 23d at Ratisbon, and on the 12th of May Vienna capitulated. In Tyrol the peasants took up arms, under Hofer, against the French; and Schill headed an insurection in the north of Germany. On the 21st and 22d of May Napoleon fought the battle of Aspern and Esslingen with ill success, but the Italian army came to his aid; and after the battle of Raab, June 14th, the Austrians were defeated at Wagram July 5th and 6th, which resulted in the truce of Znaym. On the 13th . a German youth, of the name of Staps attempted to stab him at Schonbrunn. Meanwhile Napoleon had united, May 17, 1809, the whole of the states of the church with France. Pius VII had no arms but excommunication, and this he pronounced, June 12th against the Emperor. The most important of the negociations following this campaign, was that for the hand of an Austrian Princess for the Emperor, who in order to give quiet to France, certainly wanted a son for the firm establishment of his throne. Hard as it was for him to separate from Josephine, the step was one that might have been expected. December 2d Napoleon celebrated the anniversary of his coronation at Paris with unusual pomp-a-festival remarkable for the great number of Sovereigns from Germany and other parts of Europe who attended it, and for the speech which Napoleon delivered on that day, and which was directed much more to all Europe than to those assembled. December 16 a decree of the senate, annulled the marriage between Napoleon and Josephine. March 11, 1810, the nuptials of the Emperor with the archduchess Maria Louisa of Austria were celebrated in Vienna, and April 2d, Cardinal Fesch performed the marriage ceremony at Paris. Peace had also been concluded January 6th, 1810, with Sweden on the basis of the continental system. A great portion of Europe was subjugated. Spain alone continued to fight. England remained unconquered, and Russia was still a formidable power; with America too, differences arose respecting the continental system, for this reason the decree of Berlin and Milan were revoked April 28 1811. Napoleon stood on the pinnacle of his power, which if possible was still more consolidated by the young Empress giving birth to a prince, March 20, 1811 to whom had been given the title of the King of Rome. New differences now arose between France and Russia; whatever may be said as to the causes of this war, it is probable that the chief part of these was Alexander's not adhering strictly to the continental system as he had promised to do at Erfurt. But Napoleon foresaw not the burning of Moscow, and the great impulse given thereby to the Russian people. The winter, which set in several weeks earlier than usual did the rest. Napoleon's genius, however, shone amidst his reverses, and always, even amidst the horrors of the passage of the Berezina, November 26th and 27th 1812. The battle of Leipsic on the 16th, 17th and 18th of October (1813), displayed all his talent, but its consequences were most disastrous to him. All his energies were called into action in the series of conflicts between the Marne and Seine, in February and March 1814. In spite of all entreaties of all who surrounded him, he refused to make peace. April 11, 1814, Napoleon signed the act of abdiction, and the treaty which left him the island of Elba, with sovereign power, the title of Emperor, and and an income of 2,000,000 francs. He abdicated with words. "The allied powers having proclaimed that the Emperor Napoleon is the only obstacle to the establisment of peace in Europe, the Emperor Napoleon faithful to his principles, declares that he renounces, for himself and his heirs, the thrones of France and Italy, because there is no personal sacrifice, even that of his life, which he is not ready to make for the welfare of France, and for the peace of the world." At this point we may consider the history of the Empire as, in the main, closed, and pause for a moment. He returned from Elba. February 26th, 1815, he embarked with 900 men, and landed March 1st, at Cannes, where he had landed 16 years before on his return from Egypt; and his march to Paris at this time might well be compared to his former journey. On the voyage he had written a proclamation, which set forth the reason of his return and of which he caused many copies to be made. Without encountering any royal troops, he advanced rapidly. March 7th he first met a body of royal troops, commanded by Labedoyere, who could not prevent them from joining Napoleons guards. The same evening the gates of Grenoble were opened to him. Lyons was entered on the evening of the 10th. On the 13th, marshal Ney went over to him; and March 20th he reached Paris, which Louis XVIII had left in haste. The monarchs assembled at Vienna declared Napoleon out of the pale of national law. Whilst he was exerting himself to collect and organize an army, he caused the "additional act" to be added to the constitution of the Empire, declaring that " henceforth he has no other object than to promote the welfare of France by giving security to liberty." The battle of Waterloo, defeated all his plans and hopes. He returned to Paris June 21 and abdicated, on the 22d, in favor of his son Napoleon II. This was not accepted by the allied powers' who had not ceased to acknowledge the Bourbons as rulers of France. Napoleon returned to Malmaison, and, after some days, to Rochefort from whence he wished to embark for the United States, but the harbor was closely blockaded by the English. July 3 the Capitol surrendered to the enemy and Napoleon was exposed of being given up to the Bourbons. Being prevented from sailing, he asked, July 10, the commander of the British ship Bellerophon, which lay off the port of Rochefort, what he had to expect if he claimed the hospitality of the English. An answer was sent that he had not yet received orders, but that he was authorized, if Napoleon would embark immediately for England, to carry him there, and to show him every respect due to his rank. Napoleon accepted the offer, and despatching General Gourgaud to the prince regent with a letter, comparing his own fate to that of Themistocles, he went on board July 16 and the vessel immediately sailed for Torbay, where he was informed on the part of the English government, that he was to be conveyed as a prisoner to St Helena.

On that island he lived from October 18, 1815, to May 5th, 1821, at Longwood, receiving from the English the title of "General Bonaparte," and watched by the commissioners of the allies as a European prisoner of State. Napoleon's life at St. Helena has disarmed the hatred of many of his enemies, while it has increased the respect of his adherents. He was accompan'ed, voluntarily by General Bertrand with his wife and child; count Montholon, with his wife and child; count Las Cases, with his son, who was obliged to leave him in 1817, also General Gourgaud, who returned to Europe in 1818, and by several servants. He maintained his character in the miseries of exile as in the palace of the Tuilleries. All the persons who served him at St. Helena treated him as Emperor; and he appreciated and returned their fidelity with feelings of gratitude and friendship. The Governor of the island, Sir Hudson Lowe, watched him with unsparing vigor. When his physician Dr. O'Meara was ordered to leave him, by the English governor, he remained for some months without medical aid. When he was no longer permitted to go abroad without military escort, he never left, his habitation. For recreation he played chess or some one read to him. In the confidential circle, he spoke of his childhood and his fate with the calmness with which he would have spoken of the history of antiquity. Of the French at St. Helena Napoleon was the most serene. He entertained for his son the most tender affection; of France, he spoke only with respect and love. His death was occasioned by the cancer of the stomach. He was aware that his death was approaching and spoke of it frequently and with composure. His will contains several proofs of gratitude and kindness. At the hour of his death no change was visible in his countenance. He expired—on the field-bed which he had used at Austerlitz —with calmness, in the arms of his faithful friends, Bertrand and Montholon, at Longwood, May 5th, 1821, about 6 o'clock in the evening, aged fifty-one years and nine months. May 8th he was burried in a valley of his own selection. Twenty years afterwards, October 18th, 1840, his ashes were removed to France, where they now repose—beneath a magnificent monument, in the Hotel des Invalides.

The following cronological table of the events of Napoleon's life will be acceptable to the reader.

1769. Born at Ajaccio, August 15.

1779. Sent to the military school at Brienne.

1784. Selected to complete his education at the military school in Paris.

1786. Commissioned as second lieutenant of artillery, and the same year promoted to a first lieutenancy.

1792. While on a furlough in Corsica, commands a battalion against Ajaccio.

1793. Obliged to leave Corsica, on account of his opposition to the designs of Paoli. Promoted (July) to a captaincy. Commandant of artillery at the siege of Toulon. December 19th, appointed brigadier general of artillery in Italy.

1795. 13 *Vandemiaire,* (Oct. 5), defeats the attack of the sections on the convention. Appointed commander in chief of the army of the interior.

1796. Appointed commander in chief of the army of Italy (Feb. 23). Married (March 9). Battle of Montenotte (April 11); of Millesimo, (14); of Mondovi, (22); of Lodi, (May 8). Peace with Sardinia. Battle of Castiglione, (Aug. 5); of Roveredo (Sept 4); of Bassano, (8): of Arcola, (Nov. 15-17).

1797. Battle of Rivoli, (Jan. 14); of Favorita, (16). Peace of Tolentino with the Pope (Feb. 19). Victory over the arch duke Charles on the Tagliamento (March 16). Capture of Gradisca (19): of Trieste (21). Preliminaries of Leoben (April 18). Occupation of Venice (May 16), Formation of the Ligurian Republic (31). Proclamation of the Cisalpine Republic (July 8). Peace of Campo-Formio (Oct. 17) with Austria.

1798. Bonaparte sails for Egypt from Toulon (May 19). Battle of the Pyramids (July 21). of the Nile (Aug. 1).

1799. Capture of Jaffa (March 10). Siege of Acre raised (May 20). Battle of Aboukir (July 25). Bonaparte sails from Egypt (Aug. 17). Revolution of 18 *Brumaire* (Nov. 9) Bonaparte named first consul (Dec. 13).

1800. Constitution of the year VIII (Feb. 7). Victories ot Montebello (June 9) and Marengo (14), gained by General Bonaparte. Armistice with Austria. Nomination of the commission for drawing up a new code (Aug. 12). Conspiracy of Arena (Oct. 9) discovered, Explosion of the infernal machine (Dec. 24).

1801. Peace of Luneville (Feb. 9) with Austria; peace with Spain (March 21); with Naples (28). Concordate with the Pope (July 15). Peace with Bavaria (Aug. 24); with Portugal (Sept, 29). Preliminaries of peace with England (Oct 1). Peace wfth Russia (8); with Turkey (9), with Algiers (Dec. 17).

1802. Bonaparte named president of the Italian Republic (Jan. 26) Peace of Amiens (March 25). Proclamation of amnesty to emigrants. The term of Bonaparte's consulship prolonged ten years (May 1). Creation of the legion of honor (19) Bonaparte declared consul for life (Aug. 2).

1803. Creation of senatorships (Jan. 4). New organization of the Institute. Assumes the title of grand mediator of the Helvetic republic. Sale of Louisiana to the United States (April 30). Renewal of hostilities with England (May 20).

1804. Arrest of Pichegru (Feb. 28). Death of the duc d'Enghien (March 21). The senate confers on Napoleon the title of Emperor of the French (May 18).

1805. The Emperor accepts the crown of Italy (March 18). Treaty of Pressburg between England and Russia (April 11). Austria joins the coalition (Aug. 9). Battle of Elchingen (Oct. 14), of Trafalgar (21), of Austerlitz (Dec. 2). Peace of Pressburg between France and Austria.

1806. Formation of the kingdoms of Bavaria and Wurtemburg (Jan. 1). Joseph Bonaparte proclaimed the king of the two Sicilies (March 30). Prussia is allowed to occupy Hanover. Louis Bonaparte proclaimed king of Holland (June 5). Napoleon proclaimed the protector of the confederation of the Rhine (July 12). Rupture with Prussia (Oct. 6). Battle of Jena (14). Capture of Berlin (25). Occupation of Hanover, capture of Posen, Hamburg, Bremen, Warsaw, Thorn, &c., (Oct. 28 to Dec. 6). Berlin decree declares the British isles in a state of blockade (Nov. 21).

1807. Battle of Eylau (Feb. 8); of Friedland (June 14). Peace of Tilsit with Russia and Prussia July 7 . Creation of the kingdom of Westphalia (Aug. 8). The English bombard Copenhagen. Alliance between France and Denmark. Treaty between France and Spain. Russia breaks off all communication with England (Oct. 31). Treaty between Holland and France. British order in council of (Nov. 11), in relation for the Berlin decree. Capture of Lisbon by Junot. Prussia interdicts all intercourse with England (Dec. 1). Jerome Bonaparte placed on the throne of Westphalia, Milan decree (Dec. 7).

1808. French troops occupy Rome (Feb. 2); overrun Spain. Creation of majorats and hereditary titles (March 11). Treaty of Bayonne (May 5). Joseph Bonaparte proclaimed king of Spain (June · 6). The French troops evacuate Portugal (Aug. 30). The English enter Spain (Oct. 29). War of the peninsula. Napoleon arrives in Spain (Nov. 4). Capture of Madrid (Dec. 4).

1809. Capture of Saragosa (Feb 21); of Oporto (March 29). Austria renews hostilities (April 9). Napoleon leaves Paris (13). Battle of Eckmuhl (22); Napoleon enters Vienna (May 13). Battle of Esslingen (20-22). Napoleon excommunicated. Battle of Wagram (July 5). Peace of Vienna with Austria (Oct. 14). Battle of Talavera (July 28). Divorce of Josephine (Dec. 16).

1810. Sweden acceeds to the continental system (Jan 6). Marriage of Napoleon with Maria Louisa (March 11). Holland incorporated with France. Capture of Ciudad Rodrigo. Battle of Busaco. Institution of the *prevotal* courts.

1811. Capture of Oporto and Olivenza (Jan. 22), and Badajoz (March 10) by the French. Birth of the King of Rome (March 20). Battle of Fuente de Onoro (May 4-6); of Saguntum (Oct. 20).

1812. Capture of Ciudad Rodrigo, by Wellington (Jan. 19); of Badajoz (April 7). Battle of Tarragona (June 12). Treaty between Prussia and France (Feb. 14); of alliance between France and Austria (March 14); between Russia and Sweden (24), to which England acceeds (May 3). Declaration of war against Russia (June 22). Battle of Smolensk (Aug. 16); of Moskwa (Sept. 7). Capture of Moscow (14). Evacuation of Moscow (Oct 23). Conspiracy of Mallet. The twenty-ninth bulletin announces the disasters of the grand army (Dec 3). Napoleon quits the army (Dec. 5).

1813. The French army arrives at Berlin (Jan. 21). Alliance between Russia and Prussia (March 1). Capture of Dresden by the Russians (21). Napoleon declares war against Prussia; joins the army in Germany (April). Battle of Lutzen (May 2); of Bautzen (20); of Vittoria (June 21). Austria joins the coalition against France (Aug 12). Battle of Dresden (26). Treaty of Teplitz (Sept 9). The English pass Bidassoa (Oct 3). Napoleon arrives at St. Cloud (Nov. 13). Passage of the Rhine by the Prussians (Dec 31).

1814. Napoleon fixes his headquarters at Chalons (Jan. 26). Battles of Brienne (29), of Champ-Aubert (Feb. 10); of Montmirail (18) gained by Napoleon. Napoleon retires to Fontainebleau (March 30). Capitulation of Paris (31). The conservative senate declares Napoleon to have forfeited the throne (April 2). Abdication of Napoleon (11). IIis departure for Elba (20). Entrance of Louis XVIII into Paris (May 3).

1815. Napoleon lands near Cannes (March 1); arrives at Paris (20). Coalition of the four great powers against France (25). Battle of Waterloo (June 18). Abdication of Napoleon (22), embarks on board of the Bellerophon (July 15); declared by the allies to be their prisoner; arrives at St. Helena (Oct. 13).

1821. Death of Napoleon (May 5).

RUSTAN.

RUSTAN, born at Erivan in Armenia, and was chosen by Bonaparte in Egypt from the young slaves which formed the seminary of the Mamelukes. He was designated to be about his person continually, where he had many chances to distinguish himself through his presence of mind and his courage. When Napoleon became Emperor, Rustan was seen among his staff dressed in the richest oriental costume and was overloaded with presents and favors by the Emperor. However he was one of the first to leave Fontainebleau, in 1814, and was not to be seen in Paris during the hundred days. After Napoleon had left for St. Helena, Rustan went to London, where, for a short time, he attracted attention in the drawing rooms. Afterwards, he established a coffee house in Paris, and lived in Dourdang, in the department of the Seine and Oise, where he died forgotten by all, on the 7th day of December 1845.

AUGEREAU.

AUGEREAU, Pierre, Francois, Charles, duke of Castiglione, marshal of France, son of a fruit merchant; born at Paris 1757, served as a carabinier in the French army, went from thence into Napoleon's service, established himself at Naples in 1787 as a fencing master, and was banished thence, in 1792, with the rest of his countrymen. He served afterwards in the army of Italy, in which his talents and courage soon gained him promotion. He distinguished himself in 1794. as a general of brigade in the army of the Pyrenees, and, in 1796, as general of division in the army of Italy. He took the pass of Millessimo, made himself master, April 16, of the intrenched camp of the Piedmontese at Ceva, afterwards of that at Casale; threw himself on the bridge at Lodi and carried with it the enemy's intrenchments. June 16, he passed the Po, and made prisoners the papal troops, together with the cardinal legate and the general's staff. August 1 he came to the assistance of Massena; maintained during the whole day a most obstinate struggle against superior number of troops, and took the village of Castiglione, from which he derived his ducal title. August 25, he passed over the Adige, and drove back the enemy, as far as Roveredo. In the battle of Arcola, when the French columns wavered, he seized the standard, rushed upon the enemy, and gained the victory. The directory bestowed this standard on him January 27, 1797. August 9, he was named commander of the 17th military division, in place of General Hatry. He was the instrument of the violent proceedings of the 18th Fructidor, and was saluted, by the decimated legislative body, as the saviour of his country. In 1799, he was chosen a member of the council of five hundred and, therefore, resigned his command. He then obtained from the consul Bonaparte, the command of the army in Holland. He led the French and Batavian army on the Lower Rhine to the support of Moreau, passed the river at Frankfort, and fought with the imperial general with various success, until the battle of Hohenlinden ended the campaign. In October 1801, being superceded by General Victor, he remained without employment, till 1803, when he was appointed to lead the army, collected at Bayonne, against Portugal. When this enterprise failed, he went back to Paris, and, May 19, 1804, was named marshal of the Empire, and grand officer of the legion of honor. In July of this year, the King of Spain, sent him the order of Charles III. At the end of 1805 he was at the head of a corps of the grand army of Germany, formed of troops collected under his command at Brest. He contributed towards the success which gave birth to the peace of Pressburg, and, in March 1806, had possession of Wetzlar and the country around, until of the autumn of this year, a new war called him to Prussia. The wounds which he received at the battle of Eylau, compelled him to return to France. Early in 1811 Napoleon gave him the command of a corps in the army of Spain. Afterwards he returned from thence, and remained without any employment until July, 1813, when he led the army of Bavaria against Saxony, where he took part in the battle of Leipsic. At the entrance of the allies into France, his duty was to cover Lyons, Louis XVIII, named him a peer. After the fall of Napoleon, A, used reproachful language respecting him in a proclamation to his army. Napoleon, therefore, on his landing in 1815, declared him a traitor. A. however, expressed himself in his favor, but took no active part in the new order of things. After the return of the king, he took his place again in the chamber of peers, sat amongst Ney's judges, was for a while unoccupied, and died, June 11, 1816, at his estate La Houssaye, of the dropsy.

JUNOT.

JUNOT, Andoche, duke of Abrantes, a French soldier, born in Bussyle, Grand Burgundy; October 23, 1771. He was educated for the law, but in 1792 enlisted in the army as a volunteer, and by his courage won the *soubriquet* of the "tempest," He attracted the attention of Bonaparte at the siege of Toulon, and a close intimacy sprung up between the two, Junot's devotion to his superior amounting almost to fanaticism. He accompanied Bonaparte to

Italy as his aid-de-camp, and won the rank of Colonel in the campaign of 1797. He distinguished himself in Egypt, and was made brigadier general. A wound received in a personal encounter with a brother officer, who was not as enthusiastic an admirer of Bonaparte as himself, delayed his return to France, and he landed at Marseilles on the day of the battle of Marengo. He was forthwith appointed to the command at Paris, and a few months later married Mlle Laure de Permon, and received the rank of the general of division. But his own as well as his wife's indiscretions were so distasteful to Napoleon, that in 1803, he removed Junot to the command of the corps of the "army of England." On the establishment of the Empire, Junot was promoted to the rank of Colonel general of the hussars, received a pension of 30,000 francs, and a little later the grand cross of the legion of honor; but he could not conceal his disappointment at not having been placed among the first marshals of the Empire. His dissatisfaction, his improper behavior and lavish expenditures, coupled, with his wife's eccentricities. caused the Emperor to send them for a while into honorable exile, and Junot was appointed ambassador to Lisbon, where he distinguished himself only by his ostentation. In the same year he went to Germany without permission and arrived in time to participate in the battle of Austerlitz. In 1806 he was again appointed governor of Paris and commander of the first military division; but the same follies on his part, led to the same results as before. He was sent to Spain to take the command of the army that was to invade Portugal; here at least he showed his talent as a general, succeeded in taking possession of the country in the face of the greatest difficulties, and won by his gallant conduct the title of duke of Abrantes; but his success was soon checked by the arrival of Sir Arthur Wellesley with an English army. Junot was defeated at Vimeira, and constrained by the convention of Cintra, August 22, 1808, to evacuate Portugal. Landed at La Rochelle with his troops by the English fleet, he immediately joined Napoleon, who took him back to Spain, where he was placed in the command of the 3d corps, then besieging Saragossa. He participated in the campaign of 1809, in Germany, and in 1810 was sent back to the Peninsula where he was severely wounded in the face by a bullet. In 1812, he commanded a corps of the invading army in Russsia, but his slow operations did not, satisfy the Emperor, who, instead of employing him actively the next year in Saxony, appointed him commander of Venice and governor general of the Italian provinces. This kind of disgrace, combined with other troubles, and the suffering brought upon him by his old wounds, preyed so much upon his constitution, that he became insane, and was taken to his fathers' house in Montbard, near Dijon, where he threw himself from a window and died from the effects of the fall—this occured, July 29 1813.

BERTRAND.

BERTRAND, Henri, Gratien, Count, general of division, aid-de-camp of Napoleon, grand marshal of the palace, &c., famous for his attachment to Napoleon, whom he and his family voluntarily accompanied to St. Helena. He was born of the parents of middle ranks in life, entered the military service, distinguished himself in the corps of engineers, and rose to the post of general of brigade, in 1804, Napoleon had occasion to become acquainted with his worth. From that time B, was with him in all his campaigns, signalizing himself everywhere, especially at Austerlitz, where he was one of the Emperor's aid-de-camps. In 1806, he took Spandau, a fortress about seven miles from Berlin, after an attack of a few days; and in 1807 contributed towards the victory over the Russians at Friedland and excited the admiration of the enemy by his masterly conduct in the building of two bridges over the Danube, after the battle of Aspern, in the war of 1809 against Austria. He distinguished himself equally in the campaigns of 1812 and 1813, particularly of Lutzen and Bautzen. In October 1813, he defended several important posts against superior numbers, and after the battle of Leipsic, in which he defended Lindenau against Giulay, conducted the retreat in good order. After the battle of Hanau, he covered Mentz till the army had passed the Rhine. He took part in the campaign of 1814, by the side of Napoleon, whom he accompanied to Elba, returned with him, and finally shared his residence at St. Helena. After Napoleon's death (1821), he returned from this island to France. The revolution of July 1830, recalled General Bertrand into active service and he was that year, also chosen a member of the chamber of deputies. As was to have been expected he was one of those who were sent to St. Helena, in 1840, to bring to France the ashes of Napoleon. In 1843, he visited the United States, where he was very favorably received. He died soon after his return to his country, in the following year.

RAPP.

APP, John, count of, a French general during the revolutionary war, was born in Alsatia, in 1772. In 1788, he entered the military service. As aid of General Desaix, he accompanied him during the campaigns in Germany and Egypt. After Desaix had fallen at Marengo, Rapp became aid to Bonaparte, to whom he had carried information of Desaix's death. In 1802, he executed the commission which he had received from the first consul to exhort the Swiss to a cessation of hostilities, and to profer the mediation of France in the conflict of parties which had destroyed the tranquility of the country since its occupation by the French armies. The Swiss submitted to Bonaparte's decision. In the following year, Rapp was dispatched to the mouth of the Elbe to superintend the erection of works to protect the country, against the landing of the English. On the breaking out of war against Austria, in 1805, he accompanied Napoleon, and after the battle of Austerlitz, where he threw the Russian guards into confusion by a bold attack with his cavalry, and took Prince Repnin prisoner, he was made brigadier general. In the war with Prussia, and Russia, he also fought with reputation, and in the summer of 1807, received the chief command in Dantzic, in the room of General Lefebvre. With the exception of a short interruption in 1812, when he distinguished himself in Russia, he remained seven years commander in Dantzic, which he defended after the retreat of the French army from Russia till 1814, during a severe siege, in which he displayed great talent and brilliant courage, and not till all the means were exhausted and he was compelled by famine, did he capitulate. He was taken as a prisoner of war, to Kiev. Returning to France in 1814, he was received with distinction by the King, and in March 1815 was entrusted with the command of the first corps d'arme, destined to retard the progress of Napoleon. But when the defection of the whole army rendered all resistance impossible, Rapp also went over to Napoleon, who made him commander of the army of the Rhine, which occupied the lines of the Lauter and from Weissenburg, and extended along the Rhine as far as Huuningen. After several battles with the enemy of superior force, Rapp retreated under the cannons of Strasburg. When Louis XVIII returned a second time to Paris, Rapp retained the command of the fifth division, granted him by Napoleon till September of the same year, when the army was disbanded. He retired to his estates, but soon returned to Paris. When the news of Napoleon's death arrived, Rapp was about the person of the King. The information moved him so strongly, that he expressed his feelings aloud. "I am not ungrateful" he said, and immediately withdrew. The King informed of his conduct sent for him and thus addressed him: "Rapp I know that you are greatly affected at this information; this does honor to your heart, and I only love and esteem you the more for it." Rapp died in 1821, being at the time lieutenant general of the cavalry. After his death, appeared the interesting memoires of General Rapp, written by himself (Paris, 1823).

SEBASTIANI.

SEBASTIANI, Horace Francois della Porta, French minister of foreign affairs, was born in Corsica, in 1775, and having entered the French service in 1792, rose rapidly through the different ranks to that of colonel (1799). Colonel Sebastiani took an active part in the revolution of 18 Brumaire, and, in 1802, the first consul sent him on a mission to the Levant. After having brought about a reconcilliation of the differences between the court of Sweden and the regency of Tripoli, he compelled the pacha to acknowledge the Italian republic and salute its flag, he repaired to Alexandria, and had an interview with General Stewart, in order to insist on the terms of the treaty of Amiens for the evacuation of Alexandria. To this demand the English general replied, that he had not received any orders from his court. M. Sebastiani went, therefore, to Cairo, and had many conferences with the pacha on the subject, and ordered, in coformity with the order of first consul, to open a commuuication with the beys, but the offer was not accepted, the orders of the Porte being to make a war of extermination. He afterwards went to St. Jean d'Acre, with the object of settling with the pacha a treaty of commerce and found him pacifically inclined. In November he set out on his return to France, having accomplished all the objects of his mission. He was, after his arrival, employed on various services, and among the rest, in a diplomatic mission to Germany. He distinguished himself in the campaign of 1804, was wounded at the battle of Austerlitz, and obtained the rank of general of division. Napoleon entertained a high opinion of his diplomatic talents, and named him, in 1806, ambassador to the Ottoman Porte—a mission which he filled for some years, with much ability. He established, at Constantinople, a printing office for the Turkish and Arabic languages, and by these means contributed not a little to the French influence in the country. The English having forced a passage of the Dardanelles, and menaced Constantinople, Sebastiani immediately formed a plan of defence, marked out the batteries, and prepared for the most vigorous resistance; but the inhabitants broke out into a revolt and he was obliged to depart for France. He was subsequently sent to Spain, where he distinguished himself on numerous occasions: and he served in the Russian German war under Murat July 15, 1812 he was surprised by the Russians at Drissa, but he recovered his character by his exertions at the battle of Borodino. On the invasion of France, he had a command in Champagne, and defended Chalons. April 10, M Sebastiani sent to M. Talleyrand his adhesion to the provisional government, and June 1, received from the King the cross of St. Louis. On the return of Napoleon in 1815, he was elected deputy of the lower chamber, and after second abdication of Napoleon, was one of the commissioners to treat for peace with the allies. In 1819, he was elected a member for the chamber of deputies, by the island of Corsica and has since shown himself a friend to constitutional liberty and of National independence. His lucid and manly eloquence has been employed to throw light over all great questions of finance, war, foreign politics and domestic administration, and has shown him to possess at once, the talents of an orator and the knowledge of a statesman. After the revolution of 1830, General Sebastiani received the portfolio of the marine in the Guizot ministry, and in November, that of foreign affairs under Lafitte, which he continued under Perrier. After that he filled many important offices in the government of France. He died in Paris, July 21 1851.

SUCHET.

SUCHET, Louis, Gabriel, duke of Albufera, marshal of France, born at Lyons in 1770, entered the military service at an early age (1799) and passed rapidly through inferior ranks. In 1796 he was attached to the army of Italy, and attracted the notice of General Bonaparte, by his courage, boldness and caution. He then served with distinction under Massena and Joubert, and was one of the most active and successful of Napoleon's generals in the campaigns of 1805 and 1806. In 1808 he received the command of a division in Spain, and was almost constantly victorious, till after the battle of Vittoria. His brilliant service in that country obtained him the marshal's staff, and the title of duke. After the restoration, Suchet, was created peer of France. Having accepted, under Napoleon, a command during the hundred days, he was deprived of his seat under second restoration, but readmitted in 1819. He died in 1826.

DAVOUST.

DAVOUST, Louis, Nicolas, duke of Auerstadt and prince of Eckmuhl, marshal and peer of France, born in 1770, at Annoux, in the former province of Burgundy. He was of a noble family, an studied at the same time with Bonaparte, in the military school at Brienne. He distinguished himself under Dumourier, in the battle of Jemappe and Neerwinden. When Dumourier, after the battle of Neerwinden, treated with Coburg, Davoust conceived the bold design in seizing the former in the midst of his army, and nearly succeeded in the attempt. In June 1793 he was made general, but the decree which removed the ex-nobles from the service, deprived him of his command. The 9th Thermidor restored him to the army. He was present at the siege of Luxemburg, and afterwards on the Rhine, under Pichegru. He was taken prisoner at Manheim, but was soon exchanged and distinguished himself in 1797, at the passage of the Rhine, by his prudence and courage. In the Italian campaigns, under Bonaparte, he became zealously attached to that general. He accompanied him to Egypt, where he distinguished himself by his intrepidity. It was he, who after the battle of Aboukir attacked and conquered the village. He embarked for France from Alexandria, with Desaix, after the convention of

El Arish. They were captured by an English frigate, near the Hieres. Bonaparte afterwards gave him the chief command of the cavalry in the army of Italy. After the battle of Marengo, he was made chief of the grenadiers of the consular guard, which, from this battle, was called the *granite columns*. When Napoleon ascended the throne 1804 , he created Davoust marshal of the Empire, grand cross of the legion of honor and colonel general of the Imperial guard of the grenadiers. In the campaign of 1805 , he showed himself worthy of his appointment, particularly at the battle of Austerlitz, where he commanded the right wing of the army. In 1806, he marched at the head of his corps into Saxony, and, at Auerstadt, where he commanded the right wing, contributed so much to the success of the day, by his skillful manouvres, that Napoleon created him duke of Auerstadt. After the peace of Tilsit, he was made commander in chief of the army of the Rhine. In the war of 1809, against Austria, his marches through the upper Palatinate, and the engagement at Ratisbon, were hazardous enterprises. He had important share in the victory at Eckmuhl. In the battle of Aspern, only one of his four divisions was engaged, the greater part of which, with its general, St. Hilaire, perished on the left bank of the Danube. In the battle of Wagram, Davoust commanded the right wing, to the manouvres of which, the retreat of the Austrians was mainly owing. After the peace, Napoleon created him prince of Eckmuhl, and in 1811 appointed him governor general of the Hanseatic departments. In Russia 1812, his division was defeated on the retreat from Moscow. In 1813, he commanded 50,000 men, French and Danes in Mecklenburg; but was soon besieged in Hamburg, which suffered at the time very severely. Davoust was in a critical situation, and could support his army only at the expense of its citizens. He lost during the siege as many as 11,000 men. In 1814, he published, at Paris a defence of himself from the charge of cruelty towards Hamburg. On the return of Napoleon to Paris, in March 1815, he was made minister of war. When the allies advanced to Paris, after the battle of Waterloo, Davoust, as commander in chief concluded the military convention with Blucher and Wellington, in compliance of which he led the French army beyond the Loire. He submitted to Louis XVIII, exhorting the army to follow his example, and in obedience to the order of the

King, surrendered the command to marshal Macdonald. Davoust died June 1, 1823. Firmness of character, personal bravery and a military rigor often approaching to cruelty were his characteristics. Davoust left two daughters, and a son 30 years of age, who inherited the rank of a peer.

BERTHIER.

BERTHIER, prince of Neufchatel and Wagram, born in Paris, December 30, 1753, was, while yet young, employed in the general staff, and served in America, and fought with Lafayette for the liberty of the United States. In the first years of the revolution, he was appointed Major General in the National Guard of Versailles. December 28, 1791, he was chief of the general staff in the army of marshal Luckner, marched against La Vendee in 1793 and joined the army of Italy, with the rank of general of division. In October, 1797, General Bonaparte sent him to Paris to deliver to the directory the treaty of Campo Formio. In January, 1798, he received the chief command of the army of Italy, and was ordered by the directory to march against the dominions of the pope. Being much attached to General Bonaparte, he followed him to Egypt as chief of the general staff. After the 18th of Brumaire, Bonaparte appointed him minister of war. He afterwards accompanied Bonaparte to Italy, in 1800, and contributed to the passage of St. Bernard and the victory of Marengo. He signed the armistice of Alexandria, formed the provisional government of Piedmont, and went on an extraordinary mission to Spain. He accompanied Napoleon to Milan, June, 1805, to be present at his Coronation, and, in October, was appointed chief of the general staff of the grand army in Germany. October 19, he signed the capitulation of Ulm, with Mack, and December 6, the armistice of Austerlitz. Having, in 1806, accompanied the Emperor in his campaign against Prussia, he signed the armistice of Tilsit, June, 1807. He continued to be the companion of Napoleon in all his expeditions. In the campaign against Austria, in 1809, he distinguished himself at Wagram, and received the title of the *Prince of Wagram*. In 1810, as proxy of Napoleon, he received the hand of Maria Louisa, daughter of the Emperor Francis Joseph, and accompanied her to France. In 1812, he was with the army of Russia as chief of the general staff, which post he also held in 1813. After Napoleon's abdication, he lost his principality of Neufchatel, but retained his other honors, and possessed the favor and confidence of Louis XVIII, whom after Napoleon's return, he accompanied to the Netherlands, whence he repaired to his family at Bamberg, where he arrived May 30. After his arrival at this place, he was observed to be sunk in a profound melancholy; and when on the afternoon of June 1, the music of the Russian troops on their march to the French borders, was heard at the gates of the city, he put an end to his life by throwing himself from a window of the third story of his palace. He left a son, Alexander and two daughters.

BESSIERES.

BESSIERES, Jean Baptiste, duke of Istria, marshal of the French Empire, born at Praissac in the department of Lot, August 6th, 1768, killed at Lutzen, March 1, 1813. He entered the constitutional guard of Louis XVI, in 1791, served as a non-commissioned officer in the mounted Chasseurs of the Pyrenees, and soon after became a captain of Chasseurs. After the victory of Roveredo, September 4, 1796, Bonaparte promoted him on the battle-field to the rank of Colonel. Commander of the guides of the general in chief during the Italian campaign of 1796–97. Colonel of the same corps in Egypt, he remained attached to it for the greater part of his life. In 1802. the rank of general of division was conferred upon him, and in 1804, that of marshal of the Empire. He fought at the battles of Roveredo Rivoli, St. Jean d'Acre, Aboukir, Marengo—where he commanded the last decisive cavalry charge—Austerlitz, Jena, Eylau and Friedland. Dispatched in 1808 to assume the command of a division of 18,000 men stationed in the Spanish Province of Salamanca, he found on his arrival, that General Cuesta had taken up a position between Valladolid and Burgos, thus threatening to intersect the line of communication of Madrid with France. Bessieres attacked him and won the victory of Medina del Rio Secco. After the failure of English Walcheren expedition, Napoleon substituted Bessieres for Bernadotte in command of the Belgian army. In the same year (1809) he was created duke of Istria. At the head of a cavalry division he routed the Austrian General Hohenzollern, at the battle of Essling. During the Russian expedition, he acted as chief commander of the mounted guard, and on the opening of the German campaign of 1813 as a commander of the French cavalry. He died on the battle field while attacking the defile of Rippach, in Saxony, on the eve of the battle of Lutzen. His popularity with the common soldiers may be inferred from the circumstance that it was thought prudent to withhold the news of his death for some time from the army.

MONTHOLON.

MONTHOLON, Charles, Tristan, count de, justly celebrated for his generous adherence to the fallen fortunes of his illustrious master, was born at Paris, in 1783. His father was colonel of a regiment of dragoons, and young Montholon entered the army at the age of 15. He commenced his career by serving under Bonaparte, on the celebrated day of the 18th of Brumaire, and was in the list of the officers who received swords, as marks of distinction, from the first consul, on that occasion. Appointed aid-de-camp to marshal Berthier before he had attained the age of 21, he served in that capacity, in every campaign, subsequent to that period, and distinguished himself, particularly at the battles of Austerlitz, Wagram, Jena and Friedland. During a time when the state of his health, and the effects of his wounds, did not prevent him to undergo the fatigues of actual military service, Napoleon employed him in various important missions, and attached him to his own person, as one of his chamberlains. He was afterwards appointed to the command of the department of the Loire, and was proceeding to oppose a vigorous resistance to the Russians when he received the news of the Emperor's abdication. His first thought was to resign his command, and hasten to his master at Versailles. From this hour, his fate and that of Napoleon became inseparable. He held the rank of general during the hundred days. He served Napoleon as chamberlain, after the battle of Waterloo, both at the palace Elysee and Malmaison; and, finally, with his wife and children voluntarily partook of the ex-Emperor's imprisonment at St. Helena, and continued with him until the period of his decease. He was executor of the Emperor. He returned to Paris and in connection with Gourgaud edited the MSS of Napoleon. He then engaged in commercial speculations in order to repair his fortunes. These proved unsuccessful; and in July 1829, he was declared a bankrupt. From this period, he lived in obscurity, until he once more reappeared to the notice of the public, as a partaker of the attempt, made by Prince Louis Napoleon in the month of August 1840, by landing with a small party near Boulogne, on the French coast, to excite an insurrection of inhabitants in favor of his family. Montholon was arrested and tried by the chamber of peers for high treason against the existing government, and in despite of his efforts, and those of M Berryer in his defense, he was sentenced to 20 years imprisonment in the castle of Ham—but at the end of a few years received a pardon—He died in August 1853.

MURAT.

MURAT, Joachim, the son of an Inn keeper at Cahors, born in 1771, was a man of an elegant person, spirited and active, but distinguished for the most daring courage, rather than sagacity, and strength of mind, and finally, fell a sacrifice to his rashness. When a boy, he escaped from a college in Toulouse, where he had been placed to prepare him for the ecclesiastic profession. He was afterwards a common chasseur, and deserted; served in the constitutional guard of Louis XVI; then entered the 12th regiment of mounted chasseurs; rose by his zealous Jacobinism to the rank of lieutenant colonel: was afterwards removed as a terrorist, and remained without employment till his fate placed him in connection with Bonaparte, whom he accompanied as an aid to Italy in 1796. Here he distinguished himself as a cavalry officer by his impetuous courage, and followed the general to Egypt. He decided the victory over the Turks at Aboukir, and returned with Bonaparte as a general of division. On the 18th Brumaire, he expelled the council of five hundred from the hall of St. Cloud, at the point of the bayonet, and in 1800, married, Maria, Annonciade Caroline, the youngest sister of the first consul. He was present at the battle of Marengo, and in 1804, was made marshal of the Empire. His services in the campaign of 1805, against Austria, in which he entered Vienna, at the head of the army, was rewarded, in 1806, with the grand duchy of Berg. The war of 1806 with Prussia, and of 1807 with Russia where he followed up the victories of his master, with his cavalry, procured for him the distinction of occupying Madrid with a French army in 1806. Napoleon placed him on the throne of Naples, July 15, 1808. Murat governed with prudence and vigor. His attempt to conquer Sicily miscarried. His wife, a woman of sense and character, effected much good at home, while Murat himself, was called to accompany Napoleon to Russia, at the head of all his cavalry. He was here defeated at Tauratina, October 18th. Upon the retreat, Napoleon entrusted to him the command of the wreck of the army. The Emperor accused him in the Moniteur, of incapacity of his command. Murat returned to Naples, full of indignation, and sought the friendship of Austria. He, however, once more fought with Napoleon, in the fatal campaign of Germany (1813). After the battle of Leipsic, he returned with his army to his kingdom, and negotiated for its preservation, with Austria and England. The former actually concluded an alliance with him (June 11, 1814), to which Russia and Prussia acceeded, in 1815; but England would enter only into a truce, since Ferdinand of Sicily her ally, would receive no indemnification for Naples. The situation of Murat was consequently doubtful. He advanced with his army, in February, 1814, as far as the Po, but his hesitation in attacking the French excited the mistrust of England, as much as the hesitation of England to acknowledge him as an ally had excited his own suspicions. At the congress of Vienna, the Bourbons solicited for his dethronement, and England accused him of treachery. He took up arms in 1815, for Napoleon, as was then thought, while he was yet negotiating at Vienna, and formed a plan to make himself master of Italy as far as the Po Towards the end of March, after Napoleon had entered France, he advanced with his army, partly by Rimini, partly by Rome, Florence and Modena, attacked the Austrians, and called the Italians to independence, at the very time that Austria and the allies, upon his repeated assurances in March, that he would remain true to them against Napoleon, had determined to recognize him as King of Naples. It was too late. Austria, therefore, took the field against him. Forced to retreat at Ferrara by Bianchi (April 12), surrounded by Nugent, defeated by Bianchi at Macerata or Tolentino, May 2d and 3d, Murat was deserted by the greater part of his army. May 19, he entered Naples as a fugitive. The country had now declared against him. He fled in disguise to the island of Ischia, from whence he sailed for France, and landed at Cannes, May 25th. His family went on board the English fleet, and found in Austria protection and home. Napoleon would not permit him to come to Paris. But he kept up a correspondence from Toulon with his adherents in Italy. After the overthrow of Napoleon, he escaped, in the midst of continual dangers, to Corsica, while his agent Macirone, treated with the allies for a place of refuge for him. But pursued as a rebel to Corsica, invited to return to Naples by his adherents and by traitors, and encouraged to do so by several brave officers, who were devoted to him, he determined to sail, with 250 of his adherents, to Naples, to recover his lost throne. Every thing was prepared, when his aid Macirone, brought an Austrian passport, and the permission to reside in Austria. It was too late. Murat set sail that very night (Sept. 28), with six barks. A gale on the 6th of October, off the coast of Calabria, dispersed his fleet. Only two of the vessels entered the road of S. Lucido. Murat now wished to sail for Trieste, but the captain of his vessel declared that he must land for provisions. Murat then determined to go on shore. General Franceschetti and 26 soldiers attended him (October 8). But his declaration "I am Joachim, your King." produced no effect. He was pursued. He then forced his way back to the water, and leaped into a boat to go to his ship, but was seized and carried in chains to Pizzo, where he was brought before a court martial and condemned to be shot. The sentence was executed October 13. He met his fate with courage.

VICTOR.

VICTOR, Perrin, duke of Belluno, was born at La Marche, in Lorraine, in 1766, and entered the service as a drummer in 1781, distinguished himself at the siege of Toulon, served in the army of the Pyrenees, and in 1796 was one of the most conspicuous of the French generals—was appointed to command in La Vendee, and by his gentleness and wisdom restored tranquility—in 1799 his division in Italy rendered many services. In the battle of Marengo, he sustained the whole force of the Austrian army for eight hours, till the main body of the French came up—for this conduct he received a sabre of honor. He afterwards commanded the Bavarian army, until the treaty of Amiens, when he went to Denmark as ambassador from France. At the battle of Jena. he was wounded. He contributed largely to the victory of Pultusk, and fought with great bravery and success in various battles during the campaign of 1806. Commanding

the first corps of the grand army, at the battle of Friedland, he determined the success of that day, and was raised to the dignity of marshal
on the field of battle. After the treaty of Tilsit, he was appointed to
the government of Prussia, and concilliated the good will of the
people by the equity and moderation of his conduct, during the fifteen
months that he filled that important office. In 1808, he held a command in Spain, where he added greatly to his military fame. He
obtained a victory over the duke del Infantado, at Ucles, and made
15,000 prisoners, and destroyed the army commanded by Cuesta. At
the battle of Talavera, his corps displayed singular valor, but he was
not sustained in that action; and his skilful and daring march across
the Sierra Morena compelled the Spaniards to abandon the fortified
pass of Pena-Perros, which laid open all Andalusia to the French.
Charged with the investment of Cadiz, he raised works which were
proofs against all attacks of the English, under Graham and Spaniards during his command there. He quitted the blockade of that
place to take the command in the campaign of Russia, and distinguished himself particularly at the battle of Beresina. In 1813, he
commanded the second corps, which at the battle of Dresden, carried
the left of the allies, and fixed the fortune of the day, making 15,000
Austrian prisoners. He defeated the enemy at Wachau, and sustained
his reputation at Hanau. After the invasion of France by the allies,
in 1814, he defended with unequal forces, the Vosges, foot by foot.
Being compelled to fall back before superior numbers, he frequently
faced the allies and beat them. At the battle of Brienne, he took the
village of that name, guarded by 15,000 Russians and Prussians. On
the 9th of February, he retreated upon the Seine, to second the operations of Napoleon, and defended the bridges of Nugent until the 16th.
He directed the brilliant affairs of Nangis and Villeneuve on the 17th,
and commanded the advanced guard at the battle of Craonne, on the
7th of March and was badly wounded. After the restoration of the
Bourbons, he received the command of the 2d military division, at
Mezieres, and used his utmost endeavors on Napoleon's invasion of
1815, to prevent the defection of his troops. Unable to accomplish
that object, he quitted Chalons at the very moment when they were
preparing for his arrest. After the King's second return, he was
named president of the electoral college, of the Loir and Cher, peer of
France and Major General of the Royal guard. When the Marquis

of Latour Maubourg was sent to Constantinople, in 1821, Victor was appointed to succeed him as minister of war. On the 17th of March the King named him Major General of the army of the Pyrenees. After the army had crossed the Bidassoa, Belluno returned to Paris, and was soon after succeeded in the war department by the baron Damas. Towards the close of his life he lived very retired, in Paris, where he died on the first of March 1841.

MORTIER.

MORTIER, Edward Adolphus, Casimir Joseph, duke of Treviso, marshal and peer of France. He was born at Cambray, in 1768, received a careful education, entered the military service in 1791, as lieutenant in a regiment of carabineers, afterwards became captain of the first battalion of volunteers of the department of the north, took part in the battles at Quiberon (April 30. 1793), Jemappes, Neerwinden, Hondtschoote, and distinguished himself on all occasions. In 1794, he was conspicuous at the battle of Altenkirchen, and treated with the elector for the surrender of Mentz. In 1799, he was made general of brigade, and soon after general of division. March 15, 1800, he received the command of Paris, and evinced his attachment to Bonaparte at the time of the unsuccessful attempt against the life of the first consul on the third Nivose. After hostilities and recommenced against England, in 1803, he occupied the electorate of Hanover. On his return, he was made one of the four generals of the consular guard, and May 19, 1804, marshal of the Empire. In September, he took the command of a division of the grand army; in October passed to the left bank of the Danube and was defeated in the battle of Durnstein by Kutusoff. In the war with Prussia, he took possession of the electorate of Hesse (Nov. 1, 1806), passed through Hamburg to the shores of the Baltic, occupied the Hanse towns, and conducted the hostilities against Sweden, till Napoleon, towards the end of the campaign, recalled him to the grand army, where he took part in the battle of Friedland. He then commanded in Spain, where in connection with Lannes, he took Saragossa, defeated the Spaniards, at Ocana, and assisted Soult in his plans against Badajoz. In 1812, he commanded in Russia, and was left in the Kremlin by Napoleon, when he marched out of Moscow, with orders to blow it up. After the reopening of the campaign, in 1813, he was placed at the head of the young guards, fought at Lutzen, Bautzen, Dresden, Hanau, and in 1814 in the different battles in France, and April 8th accceded to Napoleon's dethronement. Louis XVIII made him peer of France. He was in Lisle when the King fled to that city, in 1815, and informed the King of the unfavorable disposition of the garrison. Louis went to Ghent, and Mortier entered the service of Napoleon. After the second restoration, he lost the dignity of peer, but was made commander of the military division at Rouen. In 1816, he was placed in the chamber of deputies, and 1819 again made a peer. He took very little part in the political events which led to the revolution of July 1830. In October 1834 he was made minister of war and president of the council of ministers. On the 28th the following July, he accompanied the King (Louis Philippe), to the review of the National Guards of Paris and its vicinity, when he fell victim to the explosion of the infernal machine of Fieschi. The chambers signified their respect for him by voting a pension of 20,000 francs to his widow, with the reversion of it to his children.

SOULT.

SOULT, Jean de Dieu, duke of Dalmatia, marshal and peer of France, was born in 1796, at St. Armand, entered early into the army as a private soldier, and became a subaltern in 1790. He was adjutant to the division of Lefebvre, on the Moselle, in the campaigns of 1794 and 1795, and was a warm partisan of the revolutionary measures of that epoch. He was appointed general of brigade in 1796 and was subsequently raised to the rank of general of division, and as such he served with the army of Italy, and was entrusted with the military command of Turin. He afterwards made the campaign of 1799, with the army destined to combat the Austro-Russian forces and was shut up with Massena, at Genoa, where he was wounded and made prisoner in a sortie. The battle of Marengo gave him an opportunity of returning home. On the elevation of Bonaparte to the chief consulate, the proofs of courage and ability which Soult had shown occasioned his being appointed to command a corps of observation in the kingdom of Naples. In 1803, he was named commandant of the corps of St. Omers, and afterwards marshal of France, on the establishment of the imperial dignity. In 1805, he commanded one of the divisions of the grand army destined to act in Austria. At the battle of Austerlitz, he commanded the centre of the army, and contributed, by a very vigorous attack, to the success of the day. He distinguished himself also at the battle of Jena and Eylau. On the peace of Tilsit, he was appointed to a command in Spain, and on the 10th of November, 1808, he attacked the army of Estremadura, put the Spaniards to route, and seized on Burgos and Santander. He was charged to observe the movements of Sir John Moore, at Salamanca, and he pursued the English to Corunna. Marshal Soult was afterwards sent into Portugal, where, at first, he obtained some success, but was compelled to make a precipitate retreat, with the loss of his artillery and baggage. Joseph Bonaparte, having lost the battle of Talavera, marshal Soult marched in connection with Ney and Mortier, to his succor; and on their approach Lord Wellington retired into Portugal. At this time, he was appointed Major General of the French armies in Spain, and it was under his advice and direction that Joseph Bonaparte gained the battle of Ocana, on the 19th of November, 1809. He was next charged with the conquest of Andalusia, and in consequence, forced the passages of Sierra Morena, and marched on Seville, of which he took possession. After the battle of Salamanca, he evacuated Andalusia, and the French armies, with the exception of that of marshal Suchet, were concentrated at Burgos. Soult was now recalled, in order to be sent to Germany; he was, however, soon summoned back. The loss of the battle of Vittoria, having exposed the frontiers of France, the marshal was sent to Bayonne to take the command of the remnant of the routed French corps. He speedily organized a formidable force, with which, he twice endeavored to deliver Pampeluna; but the allies advanced into the French territory, and Soult was obliged to retire upon Tarbes, in order to cover Toulouse. At this time he published a proclamation, in which he discovered great zeal in the cause of Napoleon. Arrived at Toulouse, a bloody battle ensued, which led to the surrender of that city to the allies. On the restoration of the Bourbons, the King confided to Soult the command of the thirteenth military division in the government of Brittany. In December, 1814, he was made minister of war. On he landing of Napoleon, the suspicions of the court obliged him to retire from his post, but it was not till commanded by the Emperor, that he presented himself at the Tuilleries. He was then raised to the peerage, and appointed to high military command. He fought at Fleurus and Waterloo, and, on the entrance of the allies into the capital of France, retired with the army beyond the Loire, and was comprised in the ordinance of the 24th of July. On his banishment, he published a memoir with a view of refuting the charge of treason brought against him for adhering to Napoleon on his return. In 1819, he was included in the amnesty, and his military distinctions were restored in 1821. In November 1827, he was created minister of war, which post he has continued to retain during several changes of ministry. Soult was distinguished for his energy, ability and great military and political capacity. Napoleon said of him, "Soult is an excellent minister of war, and an invaluable Major General." He represented his country at the coronation of Queen Victoria, in June 1838, and during his visit to England was not only treated by the prominent individuals of that country with all the respect and courtesy due to his official station and his eminent military reputation, but was every where, when he presented himself in public, to his own astonishment, warmly, and even enthusiastically, greeted by the populace. He spent his latter years at Soultsberg, the beautiful country estate he owned in the vicinity of his native village, and died November 26th, 1852.

BERNADOTTE.

BERNADOTTE, Prince of Ponte-Corvo, afterwards, Charles XIV, King of Sweden and Norway. This prince, whose political station practically refutes the necessity of the principle of legitimacy, was born June 26, 1764, at Pau at the foot of the Pyrenees. His father was a lawyer. His uncommon intellectual cultivation, shows that he was educated with great care. In 1780, he entered the military profession, and in 1789, at the age of 26 years, was still a sargeant. When the revolution broke out, he entered with enthusiasm the ranks of the defenders of his country, and rose quickly through the steps of military promotion. In 1794, he was general of division in the battle of Fleurus ; in 1795, he contributed essentially to the passage of the French over the Rhine, at Neuwied in 1796, he served in Jourdan's army. His services on the Lahn, the blockade of Mentz, the battle of Neyhoff, the passage over the

Rednitz, the taking of Altorf, the capture of Neumark, and the advantages obtained over Kray, established his reputation as a general. He afterwards, led reinforcements to the army of Italy, and was entrusted, by Bonaparte, with the siege of the fortress of Gradisca. Shortly before the 18th Fructidor, Bonaparte chose him to carry to the directory the banners taken at the battle of Rivoli, and, in his letter, called him one of the generals who had most contributed to the renown of the Italian army. After the treaty of Campo Formio, he was appointed ambassador to Vienna. In the campaign of 1799, as a commander of the army of observation, was entrusted to cross the Rhine and invest Phillipsburg. When Leclerc was appointed to command the expedition destined for St. Domingo, Bernadotte expressed himself very explicitly against the competency of Leclerc. An alienation thus took place between him and Bonaparte—and his brother-in-law Joseph—could only bring about a kind of political reconcilliation between them. After the peace of Luneville, he was appointed ambassador to the United States, but the revival of the war prevented his proceeding thither. In 1804, the first consul sent him to Hanover in the place of Mortier and his humanity gained him the love of the Hanoverians. In the same year he was made marshal of the Empire. On the renewal of hostilities with Austria, Bernadotte led the army through Anspach, effected a junction with the Bavarians at Wurtzburg, and in this way surrounding the Austrians, contributed to the victory at Ulm. In the battle of Austerlitz, Barnadotte's corps constituted the centre, which withstood all the attacks of the Russian army. June 5, 1806, Napoleon created him prince of Ponte-Corvo. In the war against Prussia he led the first *corps d'armee,* advanced from Beyreuth through Hoff, to the Saxon vogtland, and cut off the corps of count Tauenzien from the Prussian main army. October 14 he advanced from Dornburg, in the rear of the Prussian army, pursued General Blucher to Lubeck, and compelled him to capitulate. He next marched through Poland and Prussia proper, and fought January 25th, 1807, the bloody engagement of Mohrungen, by which the Russians were prevented from surprising the grand army, and driving it over the Vistula. He was wounded at Spangen June 5th. From the close of 1807 to the spring of 1809, he commanded the French army which remained in the north of Germany. War being broken out anew, in 1809, between Austria and France, he led the Saxon allies to the battle of Wagram, and maintained the possession of the burning village for two hours, but as they had lost many of their number, the Prince commanded General Dupas to support him. But Dupas refused, because he was ordered, he said, from a higher quarter to remain in his position. Astonished at this, the Prince made preparations to save the remainder of the Saxon troops, and then hastened to headquarters to complain to the Emperor of the violation of military rules. "If his death," he said, "were desired, there were less odious means than one by which so many brave men must perish with him." The Emperor tried to appease the Prince by saying that such errors were unavoidable in so extensive movements. But Bernadotte took his dismission and went to Paris. The deputies of Sweden brought him, in September 1810, information of his appointment as successor to the throne, and the crown prince of this kingdom. Napoleon had no influence on this choice, for; when he learned, in July 1810, that the Swedish diet was assembling at Œrebro, to chose a successor to the throne, he expressed a wish that the King of Denmark might be elected. But when the Swedish deputies came to Paris, the prince referred them to the Emperor, who assured them that he would not oppose the free choice of the diet, though it should fall on the Prince of Ponte-Corvo. After the Prince was elected, Napoleon made him several promises in favor of Sweden, but their mutual personal relations, were not on that account more friendly than before. October 18th Ponte-Corvo reached the Danish castle of Fredericksburg, and on the 20th amid the thunder of cannon, he landed at Helsingborg and had his first meeting with the King Charles XI.I. On the 31st, he was presented to the diet. By an act of November 5th, 1810, the King adopted him and he assumed the name of *Charles John*. The King being attacked with sickness in the following year, he committed to the crown prince, March 17th, 1811 the government of Sweden, which he conducted till January 7, 1812, with wisdom and energy. Meanwhile, the crown prince so far yielded to the demands of Emperor Napoleon, that Sweden declared war against Great Brittain, November 17, 1810. But after Napoleon had demanded, in vain, 2000 Swedish sailors for his fleet at Brest, and Sweden refused to enforce the continental system in all its vigor, he occupied Swedish Pomerania, without giving any explanation on the subject, and the French ambassador, Alquier, at Stockholm, used language which implied that the crown Prince was to have in view solely the interests of France. When Charles XIII resumed the government, the crown Prince made a remarkable report respecting his administration and the situation of the kingdom. In conformity with his views, the decree of July 29, 1812, was issued, by which the Swedish ports were opened to all nations. This resolution, a consequence of the increasing differences between Sweden and France was justified by the crown Prince, in a letter to Napoleon. In the war between France and Russia, in 1812, Sweden refused the alliance of France, and, in consequence, of the provocation which she had received from that country, concluded a secret league with Russia at St. Petersburg. April 8th, 1812, by the terms of which she promised to send an army of 25,000 to Germany, but Russia previously pledged itself to unite Norway and Sweden, either by negotiation or force of arms. Peace between Great Brittain and Sweden, was also effected at Œrebro, July 12, 1812. Napoleon's headquarters were then between Smolenk and Moscow. Sweden's policy required the greatest possible precaution, its former declaration of war against France was not therefore made till Charles John had reached the headquarters of Alexander and Frederick William at Trachenberg, in Silesia, July 9-12, 1813. The crown Prince evidently showed that he did not wish to attack France, but only to guard the interest of Sweden, while he promised to co-operate against Napoleon's plan of conquest, several times, therefore, he urged the Emperor to make peace. For the same purpose he wrote to Ney, after the battle of Dennewitz, September 6th, 1813, certain it is, that he endeavored to prevent the passage of the Rhine by the allies, for the purpose of penetrating into the interior of France. May 18, 1813, the crown Prince arrived at Stralsund to place himself at the head of the Swedish army in Germany. His letter to the Emperor, March 20, 1813, had been without effect. He had the command of the united army of north Germany, consisting of the Russian corps of Winzingerode, Woronzow, Czerniszew, of the English under Walmoden, the Prussian under Bulow, and the Swedish under the field marshal Stedingk. By the victory of Grossbeeren, August 23, over the French marshal Oudinot, he saved Berlin. By the still greater victory of Dennewitz over marshal Ney, September 6th, the capital of Prussia was a second time saved. October 4, the Crownprince crossed the Elba at Rosslan. His march, on the 17th to Taucha, contributed much to the result of 18th October, at Leipsic, on which day Charles John acquired new reputation. On the following day, he formed a junction with his allies at Leipsic. While they pursued the enemy in a direct line to his frontiers, Charles John marched along the Elbe to Mecklenburg against marshal Davoust and the Danes. Lubeck was soon conquered, and the Danish army separated from the French, which threw itself into Hamburg. A corps was left to prosecute the siege of the city, while the crown prince, with the main army, turned towards Holstein. At the end of three months, his out-posts extended to Rissen and Fredricca, and Frederick VI, King of Denmark, in the treaty of peace which the crown prince concluded with him January 14, 1814 at Kiel, ceded Norway to Sweden. Hereupon Charles John, with the greater part of his army, proceeded through Hanover to the Frontier of France. This march however, was executed so slowly that before he arrived at the theatre of war; Alexander and the King of Prussia had already entered Paris. The crown prince of Sweden now came to Paris, and had an interview with the King of France in Compiegne, but soon left France to undertake the conquest of Norway, which had elected its former governor, hereditary King. After a campaign of 14 days, he compelled the prince Christian Frederick to make a treaty at Moss, August 14, 1814, by which Norway recognized tde conqueror as crown prince of Norway November 4, 1814. Charles XIV, died on the 8th of March 1844, in his 81st year. He was succeeded by his son Oscar I.

DRUOT.

DRUOT, Jean Baptiste, post-master at St. Menehould, born in 1763. It was he who recognized Louis XVI, in his flight through St. Menehould, and caused him to be arrested at Varrenes. In September, 1792, he was chosen member of the Convention from the department of the Marne. In September, 1793, he was sent to the northern army. In October of this year, he was taken prisoner and carried to Moravia. In November, 1795, he was exchanged at Basle with Camus, Bournoville and others for the daughter of Louis XVI, and entered the council of five hundred as an old member of the Convention. Dissatisfied with the moderate system which at that time prevailed in France, he became, with Baboeuf, one of the leaders of the Jacobin conspiracy, and on this account was arrested (May 11, 1796,) but made his escape and fled to Switzerland. He was finally acquitted and returned to France. In 1796 he was sub-prefect at St. Menehould. During the hundred days, he was a member of the chamber of deputies. In 1816 he was banished from France as a Regicide. On April 11th, 1824, a man died at Macon, in France, who had lived several years there in great re-tirement, and had called himself *Merger*. On examination of his effects after his death, he proved to have been Drouot.

CAULAINCOURT.

CAULAINCOURT, Armand, Augustin, Louis duke of Vincenza, born at Caulincourt, in 1773, distinguished himself during the French revolution, both in diplomatic and military capacities, for his integrity, courage, fidelity and address under the most difficult circumstances. He served in the army from the fifteenth year of his age, but on the breaking out of the revolution, lost his post of staff officer, and was for some time confined in prison. He then served in 1792 as a granadier, and afterwards as a mounted chas-seur, but in 1795 was restored by the influence of Hoche, to his former rank as captain. Caulaincourt, served with reputation in Italy, and began his diplomatic career at Constantinople, whither he accompanied Gener Dubayet. In 1801 he was sent on a diplo-matic mission to the Emperor Alexander, who always manifested esteem for him and confidence in him. In 1804 Caulaincourt was named *Grand Ecuyer,* and about this time was stationed on the Rhine, where he was employed in counteracting the intrigues of the English agents, and particularly the English Minister at Munich, against the life of the first Consul. With the capture and execu-tion of the duke d'Enghien, it has been fully proved that he had nothing to do. In 1805 he was made General of division, and re-ceived the grand cross of the legion of honor, with the title of duke of Vicenza. He was sent as ambassador to St. Petersburg when Napoleon was carrying on his plans against Austria. After the fall of Prussia, and the treaty of Tilsit, he was four years ambas-sador at the Russian court, and received from the Emperor the cross of the order of St. Anne, of the first class. He requested his recall on the pretext of ill-health, but in reality because he met with various mortifications from the Russian nobility, who were jealous of his favor with Emperor Alexander. After returning to France, in 1811, he accompanied Napoleon, on his unfortunate expedition to Russia in 1812, which he had firmly opposed, and returned with him in a sleigh, after nearly perishing with cold. During fourteen days Caulaincourt did not leave the Emperor's side. In the campaign of 1813 Caulaincourt was appointed to negotiate with the Russian and Prussian plenipotentiaries, after the desperate battles of Lutzen and Bautzen, and an armistice was the consequence. That armistice was soon broken and only prepared the way for the victory over Napoleon at Leipsic. After hostilities have been removed from Germany to France, Caulaincourt, who had been named minister for foreign affairs, was sent to negotiate with t allies at Chatillon, but on some success of Napoleon, he received orders to raise his claims so high that the allies broke off the conferences and marched to Paris. When Napoleon abdicated tainebleau, the duke of Vincenza was the chief negotiator on his part and signed the treaty of the 11th of April between the ex-Emperor and the allies. He continued to follow his master until his departure from Fontainebleau, on the 20th of April, and afterwards retired to his estate. During the hundred days he held the portfolio of foreign affairs, and April 4th, 1815, issued the celebrated circular to the foreign cabinets, declaring the pacific intent ons of Napoleon. After the second abdication of the Emperor, the duke of Vincenza took an active part as member of the regency, but the return of the King terminated his public career. He passed the rest of his life alternately at Paris and on his estate, occupied with the education of his children, and died in 1828.

NEY.

NEY, Michael, duke of Elchingen, prince of Moscow, marshal and peer of France, was born in 1769, at Sarre Louis, in the department of the Moselle, he was of humble origin, and, at an early age entered the military service. From a private hussar, he rose by degres to the rank of captain, in 1794, when his courage and military skill were observed by General Kleber, who gave him the command of a corps of 500 men, and in 1796 appointed him his adjutant general. He soon surpassed the expectations which he had excited, and in 1796, at the battle of Rednitz, was made general of brigade. Notwithstanding his rank, his impetuous courage often led him to expose his person like a private soldier. He contributed essentially to the victory of Neuwied in 1797. In 1798 was made general of division. As such he commanded on the Rhine in 1799, and by an able diversion at Manheim, contributed to the victory of Massena, at Zurich, over the Russians under General Korsakoff. Ney also distinguished himself under Moreau, particularly at Hohenlinden. In 1802, he was sent ambassador to the Helvetic republic. He opened the campaign of 1805 against Austria by a brilliant victory at Elchingen, and brought about the capitulation of Ulm. He occupied the Tyrol, and marched on to Carinthia when he was stopped in his career by the peace of Pressburg. In 1806 and 1807 he fought at Jena, and, after the capture of Magdeburg, at Eylau and Friedland. 1808, he maintained his reputation in Spain. Napoleon recalled him, but kept him at a distance till the commencement of hostilities against Russia, when he received the chief command of the third division of the imperial forces. At the battle of Moscow, Napoleon gave him the well deserved title of *le brave de braves* (bravest of the brave). After the burning of Moscow, he led the van of the army, and, by his masterly conduct, prevented its utter destruction. On this occasion, his ability was perhaps more strikingly manifested than at any former period. The Emperor made him Prince of Moscow, and Alexander confirmed the title on his visit to Paris in 1814. He fought with his wonted valor at Leipsic, where he received a wound, and afterwards at Hanau. When the enemy entered France, he disputed every step of their progress. When Paris was taken, and the Emperor was vacillating, Ney was the first who ventured to suggest to him that the contest would soon assume the character of a civil war, unless it was brought by a speedy termination. Thus he had an important influence upon Napoleon's abdication. After this event, Ney took the oath of allegiance to the King, was made a peer and received the cross of St. Louis. He enjoyed the most marked distinction at court and appeared entirely devoted to the Bourbons. When Napoleon landed, on his return from Elba, Ney collected considerable force, was appointed its commander, and, with many assurances of his zeal and fidelity to the King, marched against the invader. But soon noticing the desertion of his soldiers, and their inclination for Napoleon, he regarded the cause of the Bourbons as lost, and receiving an invitation from the late Emperor, he joined him at Lyons, on the 13th of March, and thus opened his way to Paris. In the war of 1815, Napoleon gave him the command of his left wing, which engaged with the English at Quatre-Brass. The charge made by General Gourgaud, from the lips of Napoleon himself, that Ney's conduct in this engagement was the cause of all the disasters of the campaign, has been fully refuted by Gamot by means of a copy of the written orders which the marshal received on that fatal day. At Waterloo, he led the attack on the enemy's center, and after five horses had been killed under him, remained last upon the bloody field. His clothes were full of bullet holes, and he fought on foot till night, in the midst of the slain. After the defeat, he returned to Paris, declaring in plain terms that all was lost. On the return of the King, Ney was included in the decree of July 24, 1815. For a considerable time he remained concealed in the castle of a friend at Aurilac in Upper Auvergne. During an entertainment given by his friend, one of the guests observed a splendid sabre. The account of it reached the ears of the sub-prefect, and it was immediately recognized as the sabre of Ney. The castle was searched, the marshal taken and imprisoned on the fifth of August. Ney might have escaped with ease, but he was confident of acquittal. He was brought before a court martial, which declared itself incompetent to take cognizance of his case on the 10th of November. He was tried before the chamber of peers, where the minister, the duke de Richelieu, was eager for his punishment. His advocate was Dupin. The twelfth article of the capitulation of Paris, signed July 1, 1815, promising a general amnesty, was quoted in his favor ; but Wellington affirmed that this was not the true construction of the article. Notwithstanding the remonstrances of marshal Davoust, who had made the treaty, and who explained it in favor of Ney, he was sentenced to death, on the 8th of December, by 166 votes against 17. With calmness which had distinguished him through the whole trial, he listened to the sentence ; but when the person who read it, came to his title—he interrupted him—" What need of titles now? I am Michael Ney, and soon shall be a handful of dust." When the assistance of a priest was offered him, he replied, "I need no priest to teach me how to die, I have learned it in the school of battle."

He permitted, however, the curate of St Sulpice to accompany him to the scaffold, and compelled him to enter the carriage first, saying, "You mount before me now, sir, but I shall soonest reach a higher region." On the 7th of December, 1815, at nine o'clock A. M., he was shot in the garden of Luxemburg. When an attempt was made to blind-fold him, he tore away the bandage, and indignantly exclaimed, "Have you forgotten that for twenty-six years I have lived among bullets." Then turning to the soldiers, he solemnly declared that he had never been a traitor to his country, and laying his hand upon his heart, called out with a steady voice—"Aim true France forever! Fire! Marshal Ney left four sons.

GOUVION ST. CYR.

GOUVION ST. CYR, Laurent, a French marshal, born at Toul, April 13, 1764, died in Hyeres, March 10, 1830. He studied the fine arts, but after August 10, 1782 enlisted among the volunteers who rushed to the invaded frontier. Being elected captain by his companions, he was attached to the staff of General Custine, and in the course of one year rose to the rank of general of division. In 1796, he commanded one of the divisions of the army of the Rhine under Moreau. In 1798, he was sent to Rome to reestablish discipline in the army, which had nearly revolted against Massena, and succeeded in this, but the commissaries of the convention procured his recall After the 18th Brumaire, he served under Moreau, and defeated Kray at Biberach. In 1801, he was sent as ambassador to Spain, and in 1802, commanded the French army of observation in southern Italy. He had proved too independent in his conduct and sentiments to please Napoleon, who assigned him to employment which gave him no opportunity of gaining distinction. In 1808, he was sent to Catalonia, and relieved Barcelona in spite of the scanty measures placed at his disposal, but being dissatisfied with the treatment he received at the hands of the Emperor, he sent in his resignation and left his post without waiting for his successor. This being considered a breach of discipline, he was cashiered and ordered to his country seat, where he remained for two years in a kind of imprisoment. In 1811, he was called back to service, commanded a corps which invaded Russia, and defeated Prince Wittgenstein at Polotzk, on the Duna, August 7. 1812; for this victory he was made marshal. During 1813, he made a heroic stand at Dresden, signing at last, an honorable capitulation. This, however, was not sanctioned by Prince Schwartzenberg, and he and his troops were sent prisoners to Austria. He consequently took no part in the events which marked the fall of the Empire. He gave in his adhesion to the Bourbons, and on the second restoration, became minister of war under Talleyrand; and again, September 12th 1817. He retired in 1821, and devoted his leisure hours to the preparation of his *memoirs*—the last volumes were published after his death, in 1831.

LASALLE.

LASALLE, Antoine, Charles Ludwig, count of Lasalle, was born in 1775 at Metz. While yet very young he was made an officer in an Alsace regiment. During the French revolution he entered as a common soldier and was Kellermann's aid-de-camp in Italy. In 1797 at the capture of Brescia, he was made *Escaderon chef*. He went with Napoleon to Egypt, and in 1798 at the battle of the Pyramids was made a colonel for his bravery. In 1801 he was advanced to the rank of brigadier general. He led, in 1805, the dragoons against Austria and contributed greatly towards the taking of Prince Hohenhole at Prentzlau. He concluded the capitulation of Stettin, and was made general of division. In 1808, he distinguished himself in Spain, and especially in the battle of Medina del Rioseco. He showed extraordinary coolness and courage at the battle of Esslingen, in 1809, and was severely wounded. He perished gloriously at the battle of Wagram. General Lasalle was a brave soldier and highly respected by his officers and soldiers whom he commanded and so often led to battle.

ERRATA.—In the second line of Marshal Soult for 1796 read 1769.